Praise for *Forever the Wild Mare*

"In *Forever the Wild Mare,* Ann Cottrell Free combines a unique setting, interesting characters, and moving plot to illustrate in youthful terms, what can be done in the nation's capital to provide a constructive program for the city's restless youth, while revitalizing a decrepit zoo. . . . there is a wealth of factual information in this book of fiction—from remote areas of the world through the pages of history and back to Embassy Row in Washington, D.C., adults and youth alike will enjoy."
—Associate Justice of the U.S. Supreme Court, William O. Douglas (1898-1980), in his review in *Defenders of Wildlife News Bulletin*

"A really good book. It has so many exciting parts; I'm not really sure which is my favorite." —Easton McAllister, Duveneck School, Palo Alto, California

"Set in the National Zoo and Rock Creek Park, with the nation's capital crowding around, Free has done a really fantastic job of creating a sort of mystical global atmosphere that ranges from the plains of Central Asia, to the soft hills of Virginia to the rugged Scottish Highlands."
—J.R. McAdory Jr., *The Birmingham News*

"For horse lovers, be they boys or girls, this is a must. For the smaller group of camel lovers it will also be delightful reading. Moreover, if you like Scotsmen, Buddhist lamas, United States Senators, delinquent boys or moral lessons—'such here you'll find.' The fact is that, with the prodigality of the beginner in the children's field, the author has crammed enough themes, history, characters and 'moralitez' into one book to provide fodder for a whole bookshelf." —Helen A. Monsell, *Richmond Times-Dispatch*

"It won't take readers long to understand why the publishers of this novel awarded it the *Boys' Life* writing award." —Mildred Ladner, *Tulsa World*

Other Books by Ann Cottrell Free

Animals, Nature & Albert Schweitzer

No Room, Save in the Heart

Forever the Wild Mare

Ann Cottrell Free

Winner of the Dodd, Mead *Boys' Life* Writing Award

55th Anniversary Edition

Foreword by Elissa Blake Free

THE FLYING FOX PRESS

Forever the Wild Mare by Ann Cottrell Free

First published in 1963 by Dodd, Mead & Company. Copyright © 1963 by Ann Cottrell Free.

Copyright © 2018 by Elissa Blake Free

The Flying Fox Press
4204 45th Street, N.W.
Washington, D.C. 20016
FlyingFoxPress@gmail.com

ISBN: 978-0-9617225-9-3

Illustrations by Sam Savitt. Cover image by Anita Huszti via Shutterstock. Cover and text design by Jon Robertson.

Printed in the United States of America

For Mother, Jim and Elissa

Contents

Foreword

My mother told me many times over the years, "Maybe some-day, you will make *Forever the Wild Mare* into a paperback." That day has finally arrived—fifty-five years after the hardback edition was published in October of 1963.

Although it was written more than five decades ago, much holds true today. For my mother, the wild and rare Mongolian Przewalski's mare served as a symbol of nature—untamed, un-touched but greatly endangered. Today, our wildlife, our oceans, our rich grasslands, our forests, and even the air we breathe are still endangered, per-ilously so. Climate change threatens us all. At the time of first publication, my moth-er wrote of mankind: "If he doesn't use a little self-control, nature will strike back and eventu-ally destroy him."

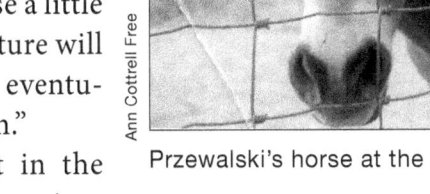

Przewalski's horse at the National Zoo, 1963

But at least in the case of the ancient Przewalski's horse, (named after the Russian geographer and ex-plorer Nicholai Mikhailovitch Przewalski) there is some good news, a second-chance, you might say. Not seen in the wild since 1966, the horses have since been reintroduced to their native habi-tat with quite a bit of success. I know my mother would be thrilled to see the photos of them once again grazing on the steppes of

Mongolia. Let's hope that other threatened species, such as rhinoceros, elephants, and orangutans, will be as lucky.

In the late 1950s a lone mare in a drab pen at the National Zoo captured my mother's imagination. She noticed her enroute home after attending a luncheon at the Zoo. She later told a reviewer, "I saw a Przewalski's horse in her pen and knew I'd have to write a book about her."

The Przewalski's mare who inspired Isabella.

As a young child, I remember going with my mother to the Zoo to visit the horse who inspired Isabella, gazing at her through the wires of the metal fence, where she stood in her barren paddock, while my mother took photographs and talked to her keepers. She was one of the last of the 30,000 year old wild Mongolian horses, alone and in captivity.

From these visits a story was hatched. Always intrigued by the far reaches of outer Mongolia, the mare inspired my mother to spend five years researching and corresponding (well before the Internet!) with a Tibetan Lama, the Royal Scots Greys, a professor in Moscow and authority on Przewalski's horse, an expert in Shaolin (the Chinese art of self-defense), and even an elementary school teacher in nearby Shenandoah County, Virginia.

My mother told *The Washington Post* in 1963, "The reason the horse survived is because it was in an area in the far reaches of outer Mongolia that are far more interesting, challenging and entrancing to me than the moon."

She wove all of this into a series of adventures led by the book's hero, fourteen-year-old Jebby Andrews, a country boy transplanted to the city, who was drawn to the exotic horse. The characters include teenage gang members, a United States senator, a Buddhist monk, a Bactrian camel, and a kilt-clad Scotsman, in settings such as the National Zoo, Rock Creek Park, and Capitol Hill.

My mother went to great lengths to ensure that every detail would be accurate, even hiking far into Rock Creek Park with an expert on Mongolian yurts.

She also drew on her background as a journalist and special correspondent in the Far East, living in China and traveling to inner Mongolia, where she became passionate about all things exotic and wild. Perhaps her love of horses, who were a recurring theme in her life, gave her a special bond with Isabella. She first climbed into the saddle at seven and was winning

Ann Cottrell Free, age 10 in 1926

cups and ribbons by age ten. She told the *Richmond Times Dispatch* in 1963, "*Forever the Wild Mare* is a converging of all of my interests."

When the book was published in 1963 it received rave reviews. It was featured in *The Washington Post* and won the Dodd, Mead *Boys' Club* Writing Award. It was also later translated into German for an edition there. Eventually, *Forever the Wild Mare* went out of print, but I am delighted to bring it back as a paperback edition. I hope you will agree with *The Washington Post,* even fifty-five years later, that it's a "rousing good story for the youth of nine to ninety."

I owe a great debt of gratitude to Jon Robertson for lending his design and publishing expertise to this project and to Evangeline Pappas for her sharp editorial skills and unwavering enthusiasm. This paperback version would not have made it into the world without the help of these dear friends. I am also grateful to Robin Robertson for her support and encouragement, to Joan Rooks who kept my mother and her papers organized, to Joan Little Ragno, who has always been rooting for Isabella, and, of course, to my husband William Nooter and my daughter Amanda Nooter, my (and Ann's) treasured family.

Elissa Blake Free
Washington, D.C.
2018

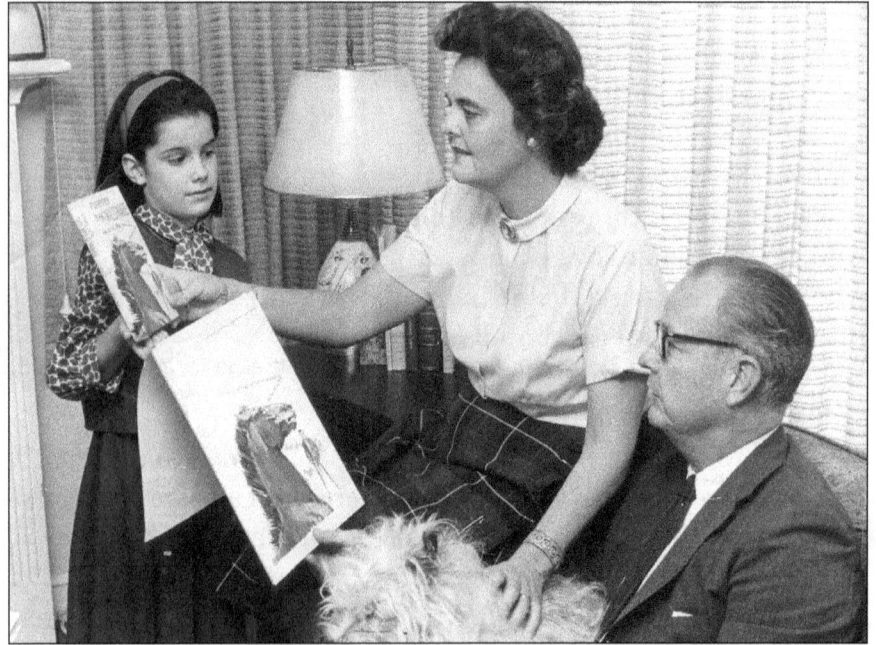

Norman Driscoll, *The Washington Post*

The Frees, in 1963, examining the first edition of *Forever the Wild Mare* with its original art by Sam Savitt. From left is Elissa Free, Ann Cottrell Free, James S. Free, and the family dog, Chips.

All of us are getting pretty far away from the basic lessons taught by nature. Shakespeare reminds us of "tongues in trees, books in running brooks, sermons in stones." One of the lessons the trees, brooks and stones would teach us is that man—regarded as the highest form of nature—cannot put himself forever above nature, nor inflict his will on all of nature, just because he chooses to do so. If he doesn't use a little self-control, nature will strike back and eventually destroy him. Jebby, the boy in this book, learned this lesson the hard way. But he was sorry for his lapse from good intentions, so he was given a second chance. All of us may get a second chance if we do not persist in destroying our wildlife, our rivers, our rich grasslands, our forests, the air we breathe and our links with the past. The wild mare, Isabella, is symbolic of all of these.

To preserve the freedom of the untamed and yet to go forward as man must go forward, that is the task for us all—especially our youth.

—Ann Cottrell Free

Author's Note

So much of so many people and so many animals has gone into the writing of this book that I sometimes feel that it is a mosaic of them all. Often they didn't know—certainly the wild mare, who inspired the creating of Isabella, couldn't—how much they helped. The thousands of animals born to run free who look at the world from behind bars instead will never know how much their plight moved me to speak up for better quarters for them, wherever they may be. And those boys and girls of our country who seem so intent on hurting one another will never know how their rootlessness prompted me to try and help them find meaningful solutions to their problems.

Swedish Georg Soderbom, Unter Sharra, meaning tall, blond brother to the Mongols, with whom he spent most of his life, helped me more than he will ever realize—just as he did the great explorer Sven Hedin. It was Georg, now with the Royal Ethnographical Museum in Stockholm, who, when he was here in Washington, could make me hear the sound of camel bells as caravans crossed the desert sands.

It was Maurice Sullivan, chief naturalist of National Capital Parks of the National Park Service, who caught the spirit of what I was doing. He helped me to find, both on foot and with a map, a possible place for Jebby, Major MacFae and Dorje Lama to put their yurt in Rock Creek Park. I will never forget the moonlight night that we followed up hill and down the kind of trails that Jebby and his friends could travel in fiction.

It was Ernest P. Walker, former assistant director of the National Zoological Park and author of the four-volume Genera of Recent Mammals of the World, who aided me with many technical details. Most of all, he infused me further with the philosophy of reverence for life.

Scientists at the Smithsonian Institution, such as Dr. C. O. Handley of the Mammal Division of the Zoology Department and Dr. J. R. Swallen, Curator of the Division of Grasses of the Botany Department, were liberal with time and effort in helping me gather and verify scientific facts. Dr. Theodore R. Reed, director of the National Zoological Park (which is a part of the Smithsonian) was also most helpful.

White-haired Charles R. Thomas, senior animal keeper at the National Zoo, shares with me respect and affection for the wild horse. So many times he has said to me, "After all these years you still can't take the wild out of these horses." Thank you for your help, Mr. Thomas.

Roland Lindemann gave me further understanding of these rare "Stone Age" creatures when I visited him and his horses at his fascinating Catskill Game Farm in New York. Many of his horses are from the Hellebrun Zoo, Munich, Germany.

Dr. Erna Mohr of the Zoological Museum and Garden at Hamburg, Germany, probably the world's greatest authority on the Mongolian wild horse, has been generous in supplying scientific and historical information. She, too, marvels that Przewalski's horse has lasted so long. She is doing all within her power to preserve the species by gathering full details about the seventy-three wild horses in zoos and preserves throughout the world. She has written a superb treatise on the breed. Dr. Mohr is my authority that Genghis Khan and his warriors did not tame and ride these horses. "Don't forget," she cautioned me, "these horses are extremely dangerous." She reports that many zoo directors refer to them as "killers."

At the time of the publication of Forever the Wild Mare, the writer believes that the Mongolian wild horse could be seen in Zoos or preserves at the following places: Washington, D.C.; Chicago, Illinois; Catskill, New York; London, England; Paris, France; Berlin and Munich, Germany; Tilburg, Rotterdam and Amsterdam, Netherlands; Copenhagen, Denmark; Rome, Italy; Prague, Czechoslovakia; Eregdan and Askania Nova, U.S.S.R.; and Shargalantui, Mongolian People's Republic.

News of the whereabouts of the wild horses still roaming free in one of the most inaccessible and mysterious parts of the world came to me from Professor G. P. Dementiev of the Zoological Museum of the University of Moscow. He is also president of the Commission for the Protection of Nature of the U.S.S.R. Academy of Sciences. He did not meet any of these horses on his 1960 expedition to the Gobi desert, but was told by natives that, up until 1945, they were fairly plentiful in certain areas. An epidemic may have thinned their ranks. But other Soviet scientists have seen a few of these horses in the last few years in areas near the Chinese border of the Mongolian People's Republic.

Dr. Rudolf Loewenthal, professor, editor, bibliographer on all matters Central Asian, has galloped mentally with me for years around the remote areas of Outer Mongolia, Tibet and China's Sinkiang. In a manner of speaking, he helped me find Isabella of this book.

When Dorje Lama decided to build his yurt out of aluminum strips instead of traditional willow in *Forever the Wild Mare*, I called on the Reynolds Metal Company for advice. Milton Morrison of that company studied the problem and pronounced that it could be done.

Geshe Wangyal, Lama of the Kalmuck Buddhist Community at Free Wood Acres, New Jersey, was extremely courteous when I discussed their ritual and philosophy with him. In fact, all the lamas I have known in my travels through Asia have been most cordial.

A former newspaper colleague, Joseph Chiang, explained the rudiments of the ancient form of self defense of the type the Lama teaches Jebby. Joe told me of how, when he was a young boy in China, his father took him to the Buddhist Temple on the hillside for the venerable abbott to teach him these techniques for self protection.

The British Embassy Library and Information Service were so

cooperative in supplying background on the Royal Scots Greys (to which Major MacFae of my story once belonged) that I could almost hear those famed mounted Scotsmen on their gray chargers shout "Scotland Forever" as they routed Napoleon at Waterloo!

Whereas I drew heavily on my experiences in the Far East, especially China and Manchuria, I cannot conclude without saying that it was like traveling all over again when I consulted the splendid District of Columbia Library and the Library of Congress. Their librarians seemed to catch my excitement about chasing down the most illusory facts.

The knowledge and dedication of humanitarians, naturalists and my editor, Miss Dorothy M. Bryan, have enriched me and I hope *Forever the Wild Mare.*

Ann Cottrell Free
Washington, D. C.
1963

1
Spilled Peas

A thump, followed by the scuffly sound of running feet, was all that Jebby heard. It happened so fast—a lightning-sharp second. He didn't know it then, but at this moment he was entering a bright new world of adventure and mystery that would test his mind, heart and muscle.

And the thump he heard was the thump he felt—wham, to the middle of his back! His feet shot from under him, and there he was, breathless and sprawled on the ground. His chin was digging painfully into the dirt and gravel outside the wild mare's paddock.

For an instant, Jebby Andrews didn't know where he was. He could have been a thousand worlds away just as easily as being flat on the ground of the National Zoo, right in the heart of Washington, D. C.—four miles as the crow flies from the Capitol's massive dome.

The fourteen-year-old boy lay there, half-stunned by the vigor of the blow—and all he could see before him on the ground were dried green peas! They were rolling aimlessly all about him and in all directions at once. One even nestled against his nose. He could feel it tickle. Jebby painfully and slowly moved his head and rubbed his eyes. Peas? How strange! Where had they come from? But even more important, who or what had knocked him down?

Before he could wonder further, Jebby realized, with a start, that he was not alone. He shared the hard ground with an elderly man he had never seen before. All that he noticed at first was that the man's knees were bare. The old gentleman was sprawled out flat and he also was surrounded by dried green peas. Not a sound came from him. Jebby sat up and shook his head, hoping that everything would come into focus. He pressed the palm of his right hand against his forehead. Ouch! How his head hurt! He groaned and looked around. Even though he couldn't think straight, he tried in a groping, stunned way to figure out what had happened. Had he been charged by a beserk wild animal? Instinctively, he turned his head toward the wild mare in the paddock. There she was, standing taut but motionless—as mysterious as ever. No, she was not guilty. As confused as the boy was about everything, he could think clearly enough to be thankful that her heels were not to blame.

After a few more deep breaths, Jebby slowly regained his wind, which had been knocked completely out of him. As his head cleared, he realized what had really happened.

It was the Caps!

While he was out flat on his face in the gravel, they had raced so fast around the curve that he hadn't even seen them. But now he could faintly hear their laughter and the sound of their heavy Western-type boots as they dashed toward Connecticut Avenue and one of a hundred hideaways. Jebby knew now what these tough boys from his class at school had done. They had charged him from the rear and one of them had delivered a sledgehammer blow to the middle of his back. That was what had knocked the breath out of him.

This, Jebby realized, was their way of getting even with him for what he had done to Shad. That bully—that yellow-haired thug!

Jebby was now on his feet, ready to sprint after them. He didn't care how many there were—as long as he got Shad. Before he started off, however, he glanced at the prostrate man, who was just beginning to stir. He might be hurt. Jebby had to choose what to do. Chase the Caps right now and maybe catch them? Or stay and help the still groggy stranger?

He made his decision quickly. "May I help you, sir?" he asked as he stretched out his hand. The man had now risen to one knee.

Jebby, as angry as he was with the Caps, was not prepared for the violence of the man's answer.

"What the blazes?" he roared. "What's going on here?" His blue eyes seemed to be fairly burning with rage. The man's fuzzy red and green tarn o'shanter that had flopped over his left eyebrow added to the feeling of fire and flame. And so did his skirt! Although Jebby had never seen a Scotsman in a kilt, he had seen pictures in magazines of these pleated plaid garments in various colors. This kilt was red and green.

"It was the Caps," Jebby explained.

The stranger looked fiercely at him, as if he were the guilty one.

"They hit us both," Jebby said.

The man didn't wait to ask who or what the Caps were. He fairly exploded, "Caps or anything else, if it's people they are, I'd call them vandals, scoundrels, barbarians."

Although Jebby didn't know it, he was hearing the Scotch burr from the Highlands at its finest—and fiercest.

"They're a gang from my school," Jebby explained. "From Winston Junior High. I'm a new boy, and they've got it in for me because I wouldn't take anything off the big one. His name is Shad. He's one of three leading Caps—Shad, Bo and Lucky."

"Gangsters, did you say?" the old man roared. "Monsters, I'd say. Safer to walk in the jungles than here. I would rather live with barbarians!"

"I'll try to catch them," Jebby said. He was still ready to spring into action.

"Wait!" ordered the Scotsman, placing a gnarled hand on the boy's shoulder. "It's useless. They've gone too far. We will have to handle this another way." His anger was subsiding and turning into gruffness. He looked at the slight, dark-haired boy closely. "A wee laddie like you, thinking you could take on those wild ones."

"I am fourteen," declared Jebby, pulling himself up to his full five feet, two inches.

He knew he was small for his age. But he was strong. His muscles were hard. And he could punch as well as the next fellow. Shad, the biggest and oldest of the Caps knew that well.

Shad was fifteen. It was less than four hours since Jebby had punched him in the nose and the eye. He had aimed for the chin, but Shad swerved and ducked and Jebby's blow landed on the big boy's nose and right eye. How his nose had bled! It went all over Shad's shirt and on the school grounds. Jebby was not a boy to pick a fight or to hurt another fellow intentionally. But what else was a new boy, like him, to do when a lighted cigarette was dropped down his back at recess? Grin and say, "Thank you?" The Caps must have expected the answer to be "yes" because they ruled the school and Shad was king.

But they didn't know boys from the country. They didn't know how strong a fellow's muscles can grow from chopping wood, reaching up and picking apples or riding Grandma's old mare all over the fields and hills of Shenandoah County, in Virginia. And they didn't know that a country boy might take something off an angry storm or a forest fire—but not from a boy like Shad.

Jebby felt he would like to tell this sympathetic man the story of the big rumpus in the schoolyard because he wanted him to know that he wasn't afraid of the Caps. He wanted him to know that they had threatened to "get him" after he hit Shad so hard in self-defense.

The man in the kilt righted his bristly tarn o'shanter, and looked seriously at the boy.

"When a man's outnumbered and the odds are against him, 'tis best for him to use his head instead of his feet or fists. So we will have to find another way to return the compliment."

"I reckon they had a right good reason to come after me," Jebby said, "but they shouldn't have picked on you, sir." Jebby's grandmother and mother had dinned it into him to say "sir" to grown men, and "ma'am" to ladies. When he said ma'am to Miss Pepper in English class the first day, she had beamed on him, but Shad glowered and then made a mock overly-polite bow in Jebby's direction. Shad was trying to make it clear to Jebby, a newcomer, that he must talk and act just the way the Caps wanted—or else.

The nameless stranger shook his head and chuckled. "Maybe it's the kilts. I wore them today for a special occasion. Your laddies here might not like the look of a man in skirts." He pronounced the word man like it was mon. "Do you think that could be it?"

"I don't know, sir," Jebby replied. Actually, he couldn't figure out why they had picked on this man either. Of course, it might have been the skirts. Kids like Shad, Bo, and Lucky didn't like anything that was different—unless they thought of it themselves. But that was not too likely.

The gentleman in the kilt, Jebby thought, was a fine sight, now that he had regained his momentarily lost dignity. He was not tall, yet he had all the dignity of one of those prophets in Jebby's Bible storybook. And the kilt, high socks and bristling tweed jacket seemed to make him more sturdy and robust. His face was weather-beaten and stern. And his blue eyes—under the bushy white eyebrows—were kind, now that he was no longer so angry. Jebby could see that this man liked to laugh and enjoy life, because there were deep crinkles around his eyes. He had a rather large nose, but it went well with his craggy face. He was a wiry fellow and had the kind of toughness some people say goes with a lightwood knot on a country woodpile.

"Aye, lad, fight we must at times," the Scotsman said. "And I've done my share of it. But this is not the time."

He paused and looked at the hoofed animals in nearby paddocks. There were zebra, deer, musk ox. Most of them stood listlessly in their pens that April afternoon, their bodies slack from boredom and natural challenges—no enemies to run from, no new sources of food to search for, no fresh-running streams to water in and no young, tender grass to munch. Spring seemed to be everywhere except in their bare paddocks. So, there wasn't much for them to do but stare into space.

"Beasts have the right to stay wild if that's possible in this Zoo," the craggy-faced gentleman said gruffly. "But man has no choice. For the right of being a human being, you have to pay a price."

The wise stranger looked quite grave. And Jebby wondered what the price might be.

"The price, laddie, is acting civilized," he said.

He glanced over at the wild mare. "Now there's one who has made her decision. She will stay wild regardless of how small and bleak her pen, and for that I salute her." His quick, palms-out salute had the style and dash of a man who was no stranger to the British military forces.

"This vanishing breed of wild horses has held out longer than almost any animal you can name. Other horses let themselves get tamed—fall into slavery—but not this kind."

These words had an electric effect on Jebby, making him forget all about the Caps and his bruised chin. This mare had been his secret pleasure ever since he had first seen her and read the sign on her paddock fence.

MONGOLIAN WILD HORSE
Equus przewalski

Inhabits the region between the Altai and Tien Shan Mountains in Central Asia. It is the only existing wild horse and is probably one of the ancestral forms of domestic horse.

There was something about the idea of a "wild horse" that had a stirring effect on Jebby. Maybe if he hadn't been looking so hard at the mare a little while ago, he would have heard the Caps coming.

Jebby had been coming to this paddock at the Zoo every single day since he and his mother had moved to Washington, about two weeks ago from the mountain country of Shenandoah County, Virginia. Mr. Mullen, the Rural Delivery carrier, had put a letter in their mailbox down the road one day not long ago. It had changed their lives. The United States government had written to tell Mother she could report for work almost right away as a secretary at the Bureau of Standards of the Department of Commerce. She had been a secretary for the government before she married, but then she stopped work. Jebby was just a baby when his father was killed in an automobile accident—he didn't even remember him—so Mother couldn't leave him to go back to work. Instead she had gone to Grandmother's little farm in the country. Those had been real happy days for Jebby, from his first steps toddling around in the chicken yard to the days he rode the yellow school bus to the county school.

But then everything changed when Grandmother died. Mother felt she could do better by Jebby in the long run if she went back to government work. She told the boy that she just wasn't the manager and farm woman that Grandmother was and that they would be glad one day that they had sold the farm—animals and all—to Mr. Belden down the road instead of letting him farm it on shares. Jebby knew that Mother was right and that she wanted to get him started in life in Washington with all of its advantages. But so far it wasn't much fun. He was lonely. Mother was working so hard on her new job that she was so exhausted at night that they didn't have much time to talk or make plans for special outings.

Jebby hated being cooped up in an apartment house in the city. The only good thing about it was being close to the famous National Zoological Park. When he looked at the animals in their paddocks and cages, he knew how they felt. And if the Caps thought they were going to make the Zoo "off limits" to him, he would—he would—well, he didn't know just what he would do, but coming to see this wild horse was his special personal business, and no one was going to take this precious right away from him.

He felt especially sorry that the mare should be closed up this way. A wild horse should have miles and miles of open land to

"This vanishing species of wild horses has held out longer than almost any animal you can name."

gallop across. A wild horse shouldn't live a boring, deadly monotonous life in a bare paddock. Not one blade of grass grew in the Mongolian mare's pen. She had worn down trenches beside the wire fence from constant walking up and down.

Jebby felt a bond of sympathy with this fascinating creature. They were both cooped up. And they were both born to run free. Maybe one day they would run free together—with him on her back. He sometimes dreamed of taking her to green pastures. He could think of a specially nice one at the foot of North Mountain, where there was a crystal clear mountain stream. She would like that water.

She wasn't what you would call a good-looking horse. She was nothing like as handsome as Bunker, the big pony that belonged to the Bryan family down the road from Grandmother's. Her head was too large for her body. She was about thirteen hands high, he figured. And with four inches to the hand, that made her not much more than four feet tall at the withers. Her legs were short and her body was barrel-shaped. Her black mane stood up like bristles on a shoebrush. A black streak ran down the middle of her back. Her color was really hard to figure out. She was not exactly brown or bay. Nor was she dun-colored, but almost. She was a tawny tan color that was different from any horse he had ever seen.

"Do you think she's really wild?" Jebby asked the Scotsman, who had taken out his pipe and started packing it. He tried to sound casual so the man wouldn't realize that this wild horse was something special and that someday he hoped to ride her.

"Aye, lad, that's what I said. You don't believe me, eh?"

"I mean, sir, is she wild like our wild horses out in the West—in places like Nevada, Utah, Arizona?"

Jebby's new friend shook his head. He had a wry expression on his face. "Those horses out West," he snorted, "are not really wild. They were domestic horses once, came here with the Spanish explorers. They are modern horses, but this mare is not a modern horse. She's their ancestor."

"Their ancestor?" Jebby repeated. "I know the sign says that, but I can't quite understand it."

"She's the only true wild horse," the man explained, "and there's a world of history in her kind. If you followed this mare's hundreds of great-, great-, great-, great-grandparents all the way back, you would have the answer to some of the earth's greatest mysteries."

The Scotsman paused and looked quizzically at this eager boy who was plying him with questions about a wild horse. Jebby's brown eyes were shining. He was listening, not only with his ears, but with his whole body.

Jebby was well-built, even though a bit on the skimpy side. He was dressed in a light blue sweater, khaki slacks and canvas sneakers. His skin was ruddy from spending most of his days up at Stoney Creek, in Shenandoah County, out in the wind and sun. His dark hair was parted on the side. He hadn't been at Winston Junior High long enough to try any of the special fancy haircuts favored by some of his classmates. He had a short nose and a wide, generous mouth. All in all, Jebby Andrews was not the kind of boy people would glance at twice in a crowd, unless they got close and looked into his brown eyes. They were bright and alert, but, in repose, they had the look of a dreamer. Here was a boy who loved action, could hold his own in a fight. His gentle side could get him into trouble because it was backed up with fierceness. He was at once both helped and handicapped by being able to put himself in another fellow's place, especially if it was an animal—a dog, bird or even a worm or spider. It was pointless, he thought, to destroy a spider's web.

Jebby was all ears now. Mysteries? He had felt that there was something strange and interesting about this horse, something he couldn't quite put his finger on. But earth's mysteries, wow!

"To find the real answers to your questions, you would have to go into regions not yet explored. Aye, son, even with all this exploring into outer space, there are a few places left undiscovered here on our old earth," the Scotsman said with a grin. "But you would have to go down into caves with caveman himself to find all the answers. You would have to turn the clock back."

Jebby could only nod his head and swallow. He didn't want to put his foot in his mouth by asking the wrong questions, even though they were tumbling one on top of the other. The white-haired gentleman continued obligingly, pausing only long enough to light his pipe.

"Aye, she's a diamond among animals," he said. "And how few people realize this. They would pass her by to go gaze at the elephants, lions, monkeys. When you look at this mare, laddie, you are face to face with a piece of the world of 20,000 years ago."

"Wow!" was all that Jebby could say.

Such talk made him forget all about his stinging palms and aching shoulder and the scratched place on his chin. Muscles that were tensed ready to spring after those Caps began to relax. He wished his companion would keep on talking. But the old man in kilts was now sorrowfully surveying the dried green peas that had rolled all over the path.

"Alas, poor Haggis!" he exclaimed in a tone of mock tragedy. "No peas for her today—or at best, very few. This sack has lived out its life."

He held up a brown paper bag with a great tear in it. When

the Caps had rushed the old man, the paper bag had fallen to the earth with a great plop and split and the peas had spilled out and rolled everywhere.

Jebby agreed that the bag was done for. "Yes, sir," he laughed, "it's a sad sack, all right." At the same time, he skinned out of his sweater and laid it on the ground.

"Maybe we can bundle up some of the peas in this," he suggested as he stooped over and gathered up a handful of peas. He had no idea why the Scotsman was so sad over his spilled peas. Nor did he know who Haggis could be. Was Haggis the man's wife? Were the peas on their way to a soup pot? Grandma had always simmered a ham bone with peas to make a rich pea soup.

As Jebby picked up the spilled peas, more questions about the wild mare flooded his mind. "Did cave men ride this breed of horse?" he asked.

The man chuckled. "Now I might seem old to you, laddie, but I don't go all the way back to the cave men. Scientists think the answer is no. I doubt if old Genghis himself could have ridden them," the man answered.

"Genghis?" Jebby asked. "I don't know much about him," Jebby admitted.

"Genghis Khan ruled half of the world just about seven hundred years ago. He was from Mongolia, just like the wild mare. Yes, he conquered men and nations, but not these horses."

This was no ordinary man, this Scotsman in a kilt. In the two weeks Jebby had been coming to the Zoo he had seen many unusual people from all over the world. Even if he could have talked to them, he was sure they would have offered him nothing in comparison with this man's wisdom. He had seen Africans and Arabians dressed in robes. He had seen beautiful ladies from India in their silken flowing gowns and red round marks on their foreheads. He had even noticed one dark-haired lady with a diamond imbedded in the side of her nose. He had seen slender, energetic Japanese taking pictures of everything in sight.

Even if he was a country boy, it had not taken long for Jebby to learn a lot about this city, just by coming to the National Zoo. The place was as full of interesting people as it was of animals. Practically everyone, he decided, came to the Zoo. But the wild mare, fortunately, was in a pen some distance away from the beaten track of tourists, and when he went to visit her he rarely had much human company. Even the Zoo guards seem to bypass this out-of-the-way area. When the Caps struck, only his fellow victim had been standing there, studying her. Jebby wondered, for a fleeting instant, if Shad and the others had deliberately searched him out, or had just happened to find him. Shad had been angry enough at school today to do anything to get even. But, in a way, it had been a lucky disaster, Jebby thought, for he was learning so much about this kind of horse and history and far-off places. Meeting the Scotsman, golly—that was a lucky break! He seemed to know everything.

"Have you lived way off in the place where these horses come from?" Jebby asked, as he finished picking up the peas.

"Aye, I've spent many a month out there, from Afghanistan to Siberia—Mongolia, China, India. Great lands, all of them. And topnotch flora and fauna and diggings." He paused and looked seriously at the boy. "And do you know that, in all my wanderings, today was the first time I've been ambushed? Luck has been with me until now." He clapped Jebby on the shoulder. "And what do you say, lad, about your bandits and brigands here in the capital of the United States?"

Jebby lowered his eyes. He felt ashamed for those Caps, treating a stranger this way! It seemed even worse that they had named the gang Caps for the Capital City itself. Because he was an American and this man was a foreigner, he sensed he must share their guilt. But the feeling passed quickly—because they had treated him just as badly. He would get even with those Caps in some way—of this he was determined! But how?

"And now, lad, let us get along to old Haggis," the Scotsman suggested. But, as he spoke, he withdrew a white card from his leather wallet. "It might be well if I introduced myself," he said, handing Jebby the card with a polite flourish.

Jebby looked at it, blinked his eyes, then looked again. It was written in Chinese!

"Oh, I beg your pardon," the Scots man said. "The other side should be up. Turn it over."

And there, in plain English, were the words:

MAJOR FERGUS MacFAE (RET.)
O.B.E., D.S.O., R.S.G.S.

THE ROYAL SCOTS' GREYS (2ND DRAGOONS)
SINO-BRITISH CENTRAL ASIAN EXPEDITION

PERTH, SCOTLAND   PEKING, CHINA

"That is one of the cards I used on my last expedition," Major MacFae explained. "The Chinese have a passion for visiting cards. They like to have you put everything—every possible claim to fame you can think of—on them. And not only in one language, but two." He grinned wryly.

The word "expedition" thrilled Jebby. To go out on exploring trips in strange places was his idea of real living. And here was a man who had really visited the mysterious places of the world.

Not having a card to offer in return, he stretched out his hand. "My name is Jebby Andrews," he said.

Major Fergus MacFae (ret.) of the Royal Scots' Greys (2nd Dragoons) clasped it firmly.

2
Haggis' Humps

The simple handshake by the wild mare's paddock put the seal on the beginning of a friendship both boy and man felt would endure. But neither spoke his thoughts, for both knew there are some things that are just not put into words. And if you try to do so, you only spoil a good feeling that rises like a magic mist around people who like each other.

As a matter of fact, Major MacFae became a bit more brusque. Even his red and green tarn o'shanter and his rough brown tweed jacket seemed more bristly. "A Scotsman yourself, eh Andrews?" he asked gruffly.

"I don't know, sir," Jebby replied. "My family has always come from Virginia." He paused a moment and wondered if he should tell Major MacFae more about himself.... He finally decided it was best to explain. "My name really isn't Jebby—that's just what everybody calls me because of the initials of my given names. I have three of them. My full name is James Ewell Brown Andrews. I was named for General J. E. B. Stuart. Everybody called him Jeb Stuart. My great-grandfather served under him. My nickname, Jeb, was changed to Jebby."

At the name Stuart, Major MacFae clapped the boy on the shoulder. "Say no more, lad. A fine general and a credit to his clan."

"You've heard of him?" Jebby asked.

"Indeed, indeed. Every man who studies your Civil War knows your Stuart, your Jackson and your great Lee. A noble young cavalryman, Stuart. A great shame he fell so early in the war." He stopped and peered at the boy, a quizzical look on his face.

"And surely, Andrews, you've heard of the Scottish Stuarts?" Jebby shook his head slowly.

"You need some schooling, boy. Not knowing of the noble Stuarts! They were our Scottish kings and one queen—Mary was her name. She lost her head, poor thing. They gave us exciting times. One day you will study them and you're in for a fine tale of feuds and fighting and all the things that make the blood boil before the telling's done."

He paused and looked at his kilt. "My old regiment, 'The Greys,' adopted the tartan of the Royal Stuarts as its own. It's much like my own clan's that I am wearing today—red and green—but it has a thin streak of blue."

"I hope we study them soon," Jebby said. "Maybe they'll be in next year's history course. I like to know all these things. And, sir, I'd like to know if you fought in any wars?"

"Not in the wars of the days of the Stuarts, young fellow," the Major replied with a grin. "That was longer ago than even I remember at seventy." Even though the Major was spirited, there were indications that he was getting on in years. His hair was quite snowy, and there were many lines in his face.

"I am an old soldier of the cavalry and my fighting days did not last long," he continued. "A bullet in my thigh forced me out during the Great War. That was World War I—long before you were born—and your parents, too. They thought I'd never put leg over saddle again, but I fooled them, I did! I went out to the East after the war. I had served there before. And it wasn't long before I found myself on the back of a good camel, hunting flowers and fossils."

"Flowers and fossils?" Jebby questioned.

"Figure of speech, figure of speech solely. I am now what you might call an explorer-naturalist."

The boy felt that Major MacFae was holding back something about himself, but he didn't know just what.

"Now come along, lad, let us pay a call on Haggis," the Major commanded. "That's what I call a worthy project, getting those humps in condition."

Jebby was mystified by Major MacFae's baffling talk, flowers, fossils and Haggis' humps!

"Haggis? Humps?" There was a question in Jebby's eyes as well as in his voice.

"Aye, those humps are in shocking shape. Dreadful!" Major MacFae replied. "Now come take a look."

"Haggis is a camel? What do you know—" Jebby was dumfounded. All the time, he had thought Haggis was a person!

"Certainly, what else?" the Major replied. "For what other reason would I be carrying a sack of peas through the blasted Zoo?" he pronounced the word "blawsted"—and somehow it sounded affectionate rather than derogatory.

Jebby couldn't think of a better answer.

"Best tonic in the world, peas. Don't know why these Zoo fellows here haven't thought of it. Fine Bactrian camel, she is. Only needs some conditioning. Peas will help."

"You mean you feed peas to camels?" Jebby had learned more in the few minutes since the Caps had knocked them down and spilled Major MacFae's precious peas than he had in the entire past month.

"Never seen it to fail," the Major answered. "On desert marches, I always gave my camels a nosebag of peas when I made camp. What kind of pack or riding animal would they be if their humps collapsed in the middle of the desert?"

By now Jebby had scooped up nearly all the peas and bundled them up securely in his blue sweater.

As the pair left the wild mare's paddock and set off down the path to visit old Haggis, Jebby knew what Major MacFae had meant in saying that bullet had forced him out of the cavalry. The Scotsman limped.

As the two approached the camel's paddock, they passed the high-headed, soft-eyed alpacas from South America. The animals rushed up to the fence, looking for a handout of carrots or any welcome tidbit. They were very gentle. Jebby wished he could get the same response from the wild mare.

"This is the first zoo I've ever visited," he confided to Major MacFae. "Back there on the farm people used to say I had a zoo of my own. Grandma used to call me 'Noah.' But I didn't have a real arkful." Jebby laughed. "Just enough for a couple of flat-bottomed skiffs."

"What did you have?" the Major asked.

"Well, lemme see now," Jebby started counting on his fingers. "I had a pet racoon, a bantam hen and rooster, a little old lamb, a pet pig that grew into such a big hog—and boy, was she a friendly, smart old thing! You should've seen her running up to meet me every time I came out of the house. Then there was the beagle hound named Beau and three tiger-striped cats. Gee, I almost forgot to mention Grandma's old mare, Windmill, and she was just about the most important, even if she was old as the hills." He paused because he didn't want to talk his new friend to death. But the Major seemed to be truly interested, Jebby could tell from the expression in his eyes.

"But do you know, Major, that next to the old mare and Beau, I believe I liked that fawn that I raised," the boy continued. "Some hunters brought her to us. They had shot her mother and they were sorry they had done it. Do you see how anybody could shoot a doe? I don't shoot or trap anything because I've gotten to know animals so well—" He stopped abruptly because he had started to say "It doesn't seem right to kill." He didn't want the Major to think he was chickenhearted. He had put up with a lot of teasing about his animals. He liked the Major so much that he didn't think he could take it if he, too, was like the others who thought a boy should show his toughness by killing animals.

Jebby was speaking from his heart—and he realized it. The words rushed out like a torrent that had been dammed up to the bursting point. He had let his guard down. He hoped the Major wouldn't let him down by not understanding. Since he had come to Washington, there had been no one to talk to this way. His mother was so busy on her new job and so tired at night he hated to bother her with his homesickness.

Major MacFae's expression softened, and Jebby could see—or maybe he just plain felt it—that the Scotsman did understand. "Useless killing is a crime," the Major said firmly. "Big game hunting just to get an animal's head to hang on the wall is sheer stupidity. Aye, I have killed animals for food or for a scientific collection, but I can't say, young fellow, that I enjoy pulling the trigger." This was a rare admission for the crusty old Major, but he could plainly see that the homesick boy needed an ally—an understanding friend. Homesickness hits different persons in different ways. He even felt a bit homesick for the days of the great expeditions in Outer Mongolia and North China when he saw the Central Asian animals of the National Zoo. The Saiga antelope—a rare creature from the heart of Asia—whose pen they were approaching now, was a good case in point.

This animal with the long, blank-looking face edged close to her paddock fence, bobbing her head up and down. She, too, was looking for a tasty handout. Her friendly bids for attention broke the somber mood of the pair. Jebby rummaged in his pockets for some lumps of sugar. Only one was left. He had brought the sugar to the Zoo mainly for the wild mare, but that proud lady had ignored the tempting morsels he threw her.

Now Jebby put his hand through the wire fence, disregarding the large red and black sign that said, "WILD ANIMALS MAY BE DANGEROUS. KEEP ON YOUR SIDE OF THE FENCE." The antelope's muzzle felt warm and soft to his hand. A look of real appreciation swept over her face. He wished the wild mare would react this way. But she seemed angry with the world!

"Come along, now," the Scotsman urged as Jebby continued to loiter by the antelope's fence. "Haggis, yonder, has her eye on us."

The haughty camel in the adjoining pen was moving her head

slowly and proudly in their direction. There was little expression in those black velvety eyes, and when she batted her eyelashes, she looked more like a Queen surveying her subjects. Behind the expression of disdain there was a certain beauty in the beast. But only men like Major MacFae, who knew camels, could see this.

If Jebby could have read his companion's thoughts, he would have known that she brought back memories of the shuffle of a camel's feet on the desert sand and the heavy, rich sound of the bells around their necks. It was a sound as bewitching in its way to the old Major as the notes of Highland pipers.

Major MacFae had always treated camels with special care. He had never believed those stories that a camel can go for days and days without food and water. Everyone called them "ships of the desert," but they shouldn't be treated like ships, rather like animals. He would never forget the tales he had heard of the shameful way camels were treated by Her Majesty Queen Victoria's forces in the Afghan wars, more than a hundred years ago! The soldiers took these animals into campaigns and never thought to feed and water them. They had stupidly believed that camels could go forever. Before the war was over, more than twenty thousand camels had perished.

Major MacFae had a soft spot in his heart for the two-humped variety of camel like Haggis. They were natives of the wilds and wastes of Central Asia—the heartland of the world, he considered it. Their hair was thicker than that of the dromedary one humper found in the Near East.

The Scotsman reached for Jebby's sweater filled with peas. "This is her third feeding of peas since I discovered her," he said.

"You mean you just found her a few days ago?"

"Aye, lad, I am a visitor here. Visiting my son at the British Embassy—and I am supposed to make a speech or two while I am here."

He looked down at his red and green kilt. "Maybe you wonder why I am in this turnout, eh, laddie?"

Jebby nodded.

"They asked us to wear our national dress at the luncheon today. The National Geographic Society was handing out medals. Such a crew we were, too—Nepalese, Japanese, Dutch, Swedish, German, and this ancient Scot."

"What's your medal for, sir?" asked Jebby. It was pinned on the lapel of the Major's tweed jacket.

"For chasing butterflies, picking flowers, following animals' tracks. I am one of those chaps who think that the answers can be found in the ways of nature. I did my field work on a camel's back all over the East. So you can understand, young fellow, why I don't like to find a camel in poor condition, wherever I may be."

"Have her humps improved at all so far?" Jebby asked.

"Can't say I've noticed any," the Major replied. "I don't expect miracles. Just give her a few more days, and she will be a fit one for riding—a proper camel."

Jebby opened his brown eyes wide. "Are you going to ride her?" he asked in a voice tinged with disbelief.

Major MacFae didn't answer directly. He declared with a chuckle, "Fine sight I'd be, riding her around in this stingy little pen!" He seemed to be avoiding a yes or no answer, Jebby thought. "She was a circus camel once and she can be ridden all right," was all the Major would say.

As the two spoke, the camel ambled over to the fence. Major MacFae took the bundle of peas from Jebby and dumped them into the paddock. "Here, old girl, have your ration—or what's left of it."

Her Majesty, Haggis, hesitated a moment before lowering her proud head to the peas, as if she did not want to appear greedy.

"How did she get that funny name—Hag-Hag-Haggis—or something like that?" Jebby asked.

"Come, lad, what kind of Scotsman will you make?" the Major asked. "First you're vague about our Stuarts and now it's our haggis you're not knowing. For shame!"

Jebby shook his head. He wouldn't even dare guess what a Haggis was, unless it had something to do with hogs or hags.

Then suddenly the Major's voice boomed forth in a dialect that Jebby couldn't understand:

"Fair fa' your honest, sousie face
Great chieftan o' the puddin-race,
Aboon them a ye tak your place
Painch, tripe, or thairm,
Weel are ye wordy of a grace
As long's my arm."

Major MacFae looked at the boy and chuckled. "Surely now, you understood every word of our Bobby Burns? He thought well enough of our haggis to write a poem to her honest sousie face. Ah, but our Bobby thought well of almost everything—mice, lice, sheep and the good Lord knows what."

Jebby still didn't know what a haggis could be—except a camel.

" 'Tis a pudding, lad—and such a mixture it is!" the Scotsman explained. "First, you take the heart, liver and lungs of a sheep and you boil this in the same sheep's stomach."

Jebby looked at Major MacFae as if he thought his friend was making up a tall story.

"Believe me, it's the truth I am telling you, lad. And if you don't like the thought of it, listen and this will make it taste better. The oatmeal, suet, salt, pepper and onions you add give it a real flavor."

Jebby didn't get the connection between the camel and the haggis pudding. Finally, he ventured to ask, "Camels were never in Scotland, were they, sir?"

"Of course not, boy, of course not." The Major lifted his hand as a teacher would. "Now I will tell you why she's named after such a mixture. Did you ever see a camel spit when it's angry? Only then will you learn of the mixture in its stomach—in fact, all four stomachs. And don't let anyone tell you that it's extra food and water they carry in their humps. It's in those stomachs.

"Well, one day, when I was on a caravan trek into the desert, blasted bandits came upon us. Mind you, now, it wasn't an ambush like your school lads pulled. Much more polite. Wanted to steal everything we had—our camels, too. But the first one that tried to take a camel from us learned his lesson. The creature can get angry as a man and as stubborn, too. He will spit up! A vile mess it was—not too different, I'll tell you, lad, from that haggis we Scotsmen have our poem about. A private joke, you might say."

Jebby was beginning to understand. This was a good idea, then, calling the camel Haggis.

"So now," the Major continued, "every camel I ride I call Haggis."

The Washington, D.C., Haggis only blinked her velvety eyes and chewed and chewed and chewed. The peas were being swallowed slowly—and with obvious relish. Her contented expression gave Jebby an idea. Maybe there was somewhere a special kind of food that the wild horse might like. This would make her happier—then maybe he could take her out of the pen and ride her!

"Maybe, Major MacFae, sir," Jebby suggested rather timidly, "maybe we could find something special for the wild horse. Kind of a treat?"

Major MacFae easily read Jebby's thought. "Ho-ho, young man, if you think you can win her heart with choice tidbits, you're mistaken! These Isabella-colored horses are killers. They're not for boys to ride."

"Killers ... Isabella-colored?"

"Aye, an old word and a good one—you never hear it any more—for a horse of this color. Goes back to the days of the first Queen Elizabeth. It's neither dun nor bay. It's Isabella-color, I'd say—something in between."

Jebby looked down at his tennis shoes, wondering whether to tell the Scotsman that he'd bet anything that this mare was no killer. A bit wild and skittish, perhaps, but no killer. He decided against it, though. Maybe he would be able to show the Major one day that he could ride her—but first he would have to make her become more friendly. Special foods might help. But—what kind?

Major MacFae laid an arm across Jebby's shoulders. "Meet me here at her paddock at this time tomorrow afternoon," he said. "I'll not promise what I'll bring." But there was a promise in his voice, Jebby could tell.

3

Isabella's Surprise

Jebby could scarcely wait for school to be dismissed for the day. Ever since telling Major MacFae good-by yesterday afternoon, he had felt that the time of their second meeting would never arrive. The hours dragged unmercifully. Finally, the hands of the large wall clock in the history classroom reached 3 p.m. At last, the triumphant bell of liberation clanged throughout the corridors and classrooms of the huge junior high school and 1,052 young hearts leaped in gladness. But none soared higher than that of Jebby Andrews—a boy with a mission.

He was off like a bounding gazelle from the broad African plain. He crossed Connecticut Avenue, charged through the revolving doors of his large apartment house with such force that they twirled dizzily for moments after he left. He didn't wait for the self-service elevator, but rushed up three flights of stairs, ran down the corridor, passing all the look-alike doors until he came to his own. His key was ready. He had pulled it out of his pocket as he ran. He entered, slammed his schoolbooks on a chair, base-slid to the telephone. He dialed her office number quickly.

"Mother, it's me!" he exclaimed breathlessly. "I am home. But now I'm going to the Zoo, just like I said. Major MacFae has a surprise. I know. I know." The boy's faith could not have been shaken by bombs or bullets.

Last night he had explained about Major MacFae and the

horse to his mother. He had told her about the Caps, too,—of how he had accidently bloodied the nose of the king of the school in front of hundreds of kids. He promised her he would stay on guard. They wouldn't ambush him again. Yes, that was the word— ambush—that Major MacFae used. A very good word. Besides, Shad had stayed home today. As well as bloodying his nose in the schoolyard fight, Jebby learned that he had given the bully a black eye. So Shad didn't want to show it at school today.

Jebby was off again. Down the steps, through the twirling doors, and across the avenue. And like a comet he zoomed through the Zoo's black iron gates. The leisurely yak, the bison and the Alaskan reindeer saw only a streak of a boy flash by. The sauntering, hands-in-pocket, lonely boy of other days had been replaced by a youth of zest and purpose.

The dreamer was about to exchange his dreams for action, for today could easily mark the first step toward taming and riding the only true wild horse. A "killer" horse, the Major called her. Those words caused chills of excitement to run up and down Jebby's back. Yes, that's what the Scotsman had said, "Those Isabella-colored horses are killers."

Isabella-colored? The name Isabella appealed to him. "Isabella." Far nicer name than Haggis certainly. An idea flashed through his mind, so bright and sharp that he knew he would never change it, not if he pondered for weeks would he find a better name ... Isabella ... Isabella. Jebby decided then and there that Isabella she should be from now on.

What kind of choice morsel, he wondered, would Major Mac-Fae bring? How many times at school today had he thought of different things that might interest the wild mare? A bran mash soaked with molasses was always a treat for thoroughbred hunters in the stables of the rich. Or perhaps it would be some kind of strange fruit. In Arabian Nights, horses and camels feasted off dates, fish and juicy locusts. He remembered Grandmother reading aloud about such things when he was a very little boy.

Jebby's thoughts slipped and slithered like shiny black water bugs on the glassy surface of a tranquil pond. Spring in the air made him a bit giddy, too, along with the thoughts of his three new friends—Major Fergus MacFae, Haggis and Isabella.

As he came around the curve leading to the wild mare's pen, Jebby's face shone in anticipation. He knew he would not be disappointed. He could tell Major MacFae was not that kind of person.

And there he was! Jebby felt relieved, because the events of yesterday had been so unusual, he almost felt they hadn't taken place. But it was all real, for here was the Scotsman as before, except for one big difference. He was wearing pants instead of a kilt. But he was still wearing his gaudy tarn o'shanter.

At his feet were two large paper shopping bags. The former explorer had been true to his word. He had brought the mare—Isabella—a choice morsel surprise.

"Fetched something along I thought our girl might fancy," the Major said by way of a greeting. His tone was quite casual, as if bringing delicacies to wild Mongolian mares in zoos was an everyday occurrence.

"Thank you, oh, thank you," was all that the excited Jebby could manage to say. His eyes were shining and his face was flushed from running.

Major MacFae reached into one of the shopping bags. Jebby held his breath…. But, after he took one look at what the Major held in his hand, he was unable to hide his disappointment.

"Hay!" was all he could say. Hay—miserable, everyday hay! Surely the Major was teasing him.

"Well, that's one name for it," the Scotsman replied. He did not seem very surprised by Jebby's disappointment. "Now, lad, what did you expect me to bring—hot hounds?"

Jebby looked at him questioningly. "What's that, sir?"

"Oh, I beg your pardon," Major MacFae said with a chuckle. "It's hot dogs, I believe."

They both laughed and the tension was broken.

"Now, Andrews, don't think that hot dogs would be so out of

place for her. After all, she's a close relative of the Tibetan kiang and there are tales of those blasted donkeys—for that's all they really are—drinking blood—pig's blood."

Jebby made a face. This sounded as bad for animals as the Scotch haggis pie did for people.

"But instead of pig's blood, hot dogs or hamburgers for this Przewalski's mare, I have brought this." He held out bunches of hay in both hands. "And to do it, lad, I had to sacrifice His Excellency, Her Majesty's Britannic Ambassador and Minister Plenipotentiary's footrest. He's not likely to arrest me, because it would cause a scandal to do that to his own father."

Jebby looked at Major MacFae in wonderment. An ambassador, he had learned, was somebody very important. Therefore an ambassador's father must be twice as important.

"In other words, young fellow, I took out the insides of a hassock my son uses. But, after all, I filled that hassock myself years ago. Never knew just why I did it, but felt that was a good way to keep botanical collections that might be hard to replace. I sent samples to museums—even your own great Smithsonian, here. But first, Andrews, let me talk to you about hay. No snootiness about hay, mind you. Grass will make more than the mare run—makes the whole world run. And you know what hay is, of course?"

"Dry grass," Jebby replied. Any country boy worth his salt knew that.

"Quite so, quite so," the Scotsman replied. "But think of the various kinds of grasses. There are hundreds of different kinds of soil, but only certain ones make good hay."

Jebby remembered clover hay, alfalfa, cowpea, Timothy, redtop and Lespedeza. He could think of even more, if he tried.

"Some grasses can kill a horse or livestock," Major MacFae continued. "Take foxtail weeds. They will kill a horse almost right away. Then there are others that give special energy and strength."

If the hay would give Isabella a little extra spirit or make her more pleasant, there might be some reason for giving it to her, Jebby thought. But he was too polite to say anything like this out loud. He didn't blame her for being indifferent. He would be, too, after being penned up in one place for years.

Major MacFae ignored Jebby's sober mood. "Now consider these Mongolian grasses. I have a real mixture here, made from camel sage, derris grass and things you'd never imagine," he explained. Some of the pieces of hay were yellowish green and about twelve inches in length, with seedheads one inch long. Others were coarse and looked like weeds.

"But I thought it was mostly desert in Mongolia," Jebby said. "Mother and I looked it up in the atlas last night and read about it in the encyclopedia. I wanted to know more about that conqueror Genghis Khan you talked about. But anyway, it looked like it was pretty much desert out there. Gobi desert, they call it."

"Nearly everyone thinks that. The Gobi is a desert—and a big one. There's no mistaking that. But we have our Mongolian grasslands, our forests. Aye, flowers, too. Bluebells, buttercups...."

Major MacFae could not deny the existence of the vast arid space between China and the capital of Mongolia, where the sand is so dry and windswept that even unhatched eggs of dinosaurs lay there for centuries and centuries undisturbed by man. He could have described the flaming, almost frightening, cliffs to the west. And he could have told the boy of the sandswept ancient capital of Mongolia, Karakorum, meaning black stone. He could have talked for hours about the camel caravans that traveled, sometimes one thousand camels strong, carrying tea, furs, splendid rugs. He could have pictured for him the Tess horses coming in from the western plains, the itinerant Buddhist lamas and their temples and especially their obos, which are piles of stones, where they worship. He might even have told tales of the legendary ologor horai, the seven-inch snake whose very look could kill. But, instead, Major MacFae talked of the grass that is the key to life in this distant land, as it is in all lands.

"Horses and sheep and camels grow strong on grass," he said. "Do you know that a grass-fed Mongolian pony can give cards and spades to ponies that have been fed grain? Of course, these are not wild horses. Special races have been held just to prove that point. But here now, let us not talk about Mongolian grass and what it will do," he checked himself in his dissertation. "Let us try the Mongolian mare on a few specimens from my collection."

So, without further ado, Major MacFae, limping slightly, walked over to the mare's fence. She glanced at him scornfully as he pushed some of the hay through the fence, then waited.

The mare didn't move a muscle.

After a while, Jebby stuffed another handful of the hay through the fence openings. He whistled softly—the whistle used by all horse lovers. It sounded like "here-here-here-here."

The mare continued to ignore man, boy and hay.

"Let's not stare at her," Major MacFae advised. They walked away from the paddock.

Curiosity finally overcame aloofness. The mare moved over to the pile of hay. She lowered her head and poked it with her muzzle. That part of her head was a much lighter shade of tan than the rest of her body. It was almost white.

She nuzzled the hay again. Then she raised her large head and flattened her ears. She looked disturbed—but she didn't move away from the hay. She put her head down once again.

Jebby could feel his muscles tensing. This was the crucial moment. Would she eat it?

Yes! She took a small nibble.

"Look, Major MacFae, look!" he cried softly.

The mare pawed at the hay with a front hoof, bobbing her head up and down. Jebby had never seen her so frisky. Then, suddenly, the spring afternoon quiet was shattered by her shrill, high-pitched neighing. It even brought a Zoo attendant, who was cleaning a nearby pen, over to Isabella's paddock. He stood and watched for a while, shaking his head over such a performance, before returning to his duties.

The wild mare stopped as suddenly as she had started, lowered her head again and tossed the grass in the air with a kind of abandon.

After a while, Jebby stuffed another handful of hay through the fence openings. He whistled softly—

Jebby rushed to the fence to watch more closely.

She repeated the performance, neighing in the same high-pitched way.

In a little while, she quieted down, looked at the Mongolian-grown hay and began to eat once more. She no longer gingerly nibbled, but ate in a normal, even eager fashion.

"Well, there goes my collection—even some of that Mongolian rhubarb that Marco Polo wrote about," Major MacFae said, half to himself, "but it's worth it." He didn't really mind seeing the fodder disappear, for the grass from the Asian steppe and the mare from the Asian steppe belonged together. Both, in a fashion, were exiles from their native land. It was better to have the grass inside the horse, instead of inside the British Ambassador's hassock. "We've seen something rather interesting, Andrews," he declared, "a case of genetic memory."

"What's that, sir?" Jebby was puzzled. He had a vague recollection about genetics from seventh grade science class. It was when they studied some biology. But he was never really sure of what it was all about—something about things called chromosomes and people with different colored eyes. He should have paid closer attention to Miss West and not thought so much about getting back to his "critters" on the farm.

"I'll try to explain," the Major said. "This Mongolian grass has nourished these wild horses for so many centuries that the minerals in it have helped to produce them. The grass, you might say, was the horse. I think this mare inherited a taste for the stuff."

The naturalist-explorer shook his head in amazement over his own discovery. "By Jove, it's really remarkable when you think about it," he continued. "This mare has never been near Mongolia—Inner or Outer—and those out-of-the-way, sandy, scrubby spots where her kind breed. You know, they've been pushed further and further back toward China, into the wasteland, by domestic herds of horses, and sheep. She's at least three generations away from those remarkable little herds rounded up in the year 1902, I believe it was. But to get back to my story, Andrews, look at how that mare carried on. Like a daft cat in a bit of catnip. Some ancient memory stirred up, no doubt about it." Major MacFae was in the grip of creative thinking. He was bringing together into one point knowledge gleaned from a lifetime of studying the whys and ways of this world and the living things upon it. "Although I can't figure which of the grasses—or hay—did it, she has certainly inherited a taste for this stuff. That's what I mean by genetic memory."

"Gosh!" was all Jebby could say. "We studied something about this gen- gen- genetics," he stumbled over the word, "at school. I got C on that science course. But it didn't seem like this."

"It's not easy to explain," Major MacFae replied. He pushed his fuzzy tarn o'shanter back on his head a little bit before going on. "Genetic comes from the word gene. If you know that genes are those tiny little particles of us that go down from one generation to the other, then you will understand what I mean. My son, for example, has a nose very much like mine—too large. And I had the same nose of my grandfather and so on back to the first MacFaes, who used to call themselves MacFie. These noses are the sign of the clan, whether called MacFae or MacFie. It's a gene that's doing it—no doubt about it. Not so bad for us men to have these noses, but it's a trifle hard on the lassies." He chuckled as he tweaked the end of his own big nose.

Jebby began to understand the role of genes in human heredity.

"And so it is with these horses," the Scotsman continued. "They inherit the same markings, generation after generation— same black brush mane, same dark legs, same barrel body. That mare looks just the same as her ancestors of the Stone Age and she probably feels the same, too."

"But how do we know she looks the same as her ancestors of the Stone Age?" Jebby asked.

"Ah, you've put your finger on it! Good question, Andrews. We know because cave men painted her picture on the walls of their caves," the Major replied.

Jebby became more excited than ever. He knew now what Major MacFae had meant yesterday when he said you would have to go inside the earth to find the answers to this mare's identity. Several pieces were beginning to fall into place, but there were still missing parts to the puzzle of this strange mare that the Major insisted was a killer. He was beginning to understand about the grass. That grass had maintained this blood line for many, many years. And this horse had inherited from her ancestors a taste for it.

"I understand now what you mean about the genetic memory," Jebby said, turning eagerly to Major MacFae, "but now I want to know—"

His mind was filled with pictures of cave men and wild horses—a wonderful new world of mystery. This was the world he wanted to explore—

But it was then that the Caps attacked again!

Jebby turned to face Shad. He could only shout a warning to Major MacFae. "Watch out, they're here again!" before his breath was nearly cut off. But even in that split second he noticed that Shad's eye was purple black and his face was flushed with anger.

4
The Lama Saves the Day

So Jebby's dream of cave men and prehistoric horses came to an abrupt end....

The heavy blow that brought this about had the force of a pile driver. Next, a muscular arm grabbed him around his neck. As it tightened, Jebby's breath was almost cut off and his body was bent back against the leather-jacketed boy who held him. He wriggled and struggled hard against Shad's grip, but the older boy's arm was strong and Jebby couldn't wrest free. Then, Shad hit him again in the middle of his back. Jebby continued to strain against Shad's arm. But after that last blow, he couldn't gather his strength or even his senses. Everything was all mixed up—very mixed up.... And now he could feel himself sliding to the ground. The blurred shape of the wild horse was swimming in front of his eyes. She seemed so distant, so much a part of a dream world. He was slipping and gasping for breath all at the same time, for Shad was relaxing his grip and letting him fall. The yellow spice bushes that had appeared so bright and full of spring began to fade before his eyes before he hit the gravel path. All he could hear was Shad's voice—but it seemed to be thin and far away.

"I've got you now," Shad rasped.

But Shad was wrong. Maybe it was the impact of hitting the ground that shocked Jebby into reality. Or it could have been those quick breaths that he was taking that were clearing his head.

Anyway, Jebby wasn't down for long. He was rising to his feet. As he did so, he quickly turned and tried to grab Shad around the knees, to throw him down. But the bigger boy was too quick for him. He socked Jebby in the jaw. Shad was strong and the blow was well aimed. Jebby fell back again to the ground. Shad, furious that he had almost been pulled off balance, suddenly flung his whole weight against his smaller antagonist. Jebby could feel the older boy's warm breath, and the touch of his messed-up yellow hair that flopped over his face. Jebby began pushing against Shad—and kept the gang leader from completely pinning him down. There was still a little space between Jebby's shoulders and the ground, so Shad kept pushing. But the country boy was holding the other off by pure will power and muscle, for Jebby was pushing, pushing, pushing, too. A tiny space—like a crack of daylight coming into a darkened room—was opening up between them. It was widening.... Now, this was Jebby's big moment! He summoned up what felt like the final ounce of strength, somehow drew his right leg up to his chest—and kicked!

His foot struck something hard. It landed on the buckle of Shad's wide leather belt. This was the kind of belt worn by motorcycle riders. It was studded with metal. The kick eased Shad's weight, but only for an instant.... And it didn't give Jebby time enough to scramble to his feet.

Shad seemed to be fairly hissing with rage as he flung himself at Jebby again. His face, if possible, was even redder than when he began the attack. His right eye was closed shut from Jebby's blow of the day before and his other eye seemed a narrow slit. This time, as Shad came at him, Jebby sensed there was something different in the fight. But he didn't know what it was. No time for thinking now. From the expression on Shad's face, Jebby could see that his opponent was going to hold him down and really give him a beating. Even with every muscle and nerve straining, Jebby felt powerless. He twisted. He tried to turn. But Shad's weight was pinning him down.

No! No ... no ... was all Jebby could think. That boy wasn't going to make him yell for mercy. He wasn't going to waste his strength in cries. He wasn't going to be beaten. He had done nothing wrong and he wasn't going to let this happen to him. Jebby's face was growing red and the veins stood out like cords. His blood was pounding in his temples. He was determined never to give up, but Shad was grabbing his wrists, trying to bend his arms over his head. No! No ... Jebby closed his eyes, clenched his teeth and once more pushed with muscle, fibre, bone, muscle. He was all instinct now. This seemed the longest moment....

And then, suddenly, there was a feeling of lightness ... a feeling of release ... a feeling of liberation. Had he succeeded? He didn't believe he had thrown off the heavy, enraged boy. How had he done it?

Then he knew.... A hand had come between the two antagonists, like a magic wand.

Shad's wrist was strongly grasped by a small, delicate hand. It was as finely shaped as a woman's, and it was the color of old ivory. The hand was bending the assailant's wrist back, back and further back until Jebby could see the veins standing out hard and blue. The other boy seemed to be lifted from Jebby as his whole body was pulled back by the strong ivory hand.

Jebby's body was now free of Shad's weight because the bigger boy had been lifted into the air and cast aside like an old orange peel.

Jebby lay there, exhausted, but he was able to take his first good look at his rescuer. He was a slight little man in a dark blue suit. His face, too, was the color of yellowed old ivory. He wore steel-rimmed spectacles. And he looked as if his entire life might have been passed bending over books in a library, instead of handling tough junior-high-school boys as if they were pieces of fluff!

Jebby summoned all his strength to get up and to speak. But before they could exchange a word, the little man turned to Major MacFae, who was holding the towheaded boy called Bo by the collar. The boy's sweater and shirt were bunched up in the tight grip of the Scotsman's hand.

An angry and scornful Major MacFae finally flung him aside, as he cautioned in a cold, stern voice, "Don't ever try this again! You should be behind bars." Then he paused and turned his piercing blue eyes on the cowering boy.

"What ails you? Is devil's fire burning you?" His Scotch burr was so crisp that each word stood apart like icicles, cold and contemptuous of their targets.

Bo and Shad did not answer. They turned and ran away—defeated and cowed. But Jebby knew that this was not the end between them and him. The pair would avenge this defeat.

Major MacFae and the stranger greeted each other, but, instead of shaking hands, Jebby noticed that each man had placed the palms of his hands together, as if he were about to say his prayers. The two bobbed their heads up and down and their hands, also.

"Mendi, mendi," the little man said.

"Amer han sain baino," Major MacFae replied.

They both looked at Jebby. Major MacFae reached over and clapped the disheveled boy on the shoulders. "You defended yourself well and bravely, son. Sorry I was so involved with the other rascal—brigand," Major MacFae could never find words to describe any of the Caps, "that I couldn't help you. But you were under a lucky star." He looked meaningfully at Jebby's rescuer and announced, "This is Dorje Lama."

The slender little man, whom Jebby realized was Asian, placed his palms together in the same greeting he had used for the Scotsman.

Jebby instinctively stuck out his hand.

"Buddhist Lamas don't shake hands, Andrews," the Major cautioned. "Greet him the same way he is greeting you." Then he added, "A lama is a priest."

Jebby placed his palms together, finger tips pointing skyward and greeted the Lama in the fashion used throughout the Buddhist nations of the world.

"Thank you, Mr. Lama," Jebby said, "for what you did. Golly, but you must be mighty strong to bend Shad's wrist that way."

"Not so strong," the Lama replied, "but have special way of bending arm."

Jebby was in the dark as to exactly who this lama man could be, but Major MacFae soon offered an explanation.

"Dorje Lama comes from near the native place of the wild horse. He can tell you more than I ever could. I asked him to meet us here today. He is helping your government—and also mine—with maps and other work. Dorje Lama is a refugee scholar from Tibet and Mongolia."

The Lama's scholarship was of little interest to Jebby. He wanted to know more about the Lama's mysterious, effortless strength.

"That Shad is a creep. Strong, too," Jebby said. "But you knew how to handle him. How did you do it exactly—flip him through the air that way, I mean?"

"Bad, very bad, young boys fight," Dorje Lama said. "Boys and men should live in peace. Fighting no good."

Major MacFae entered the conversation. "Buddhists are men of peace. One word you hear so often in Dorje Lama's land is 'Amero.' It means 'peace.'"

"But," Jebby questioned the Lama, "how did you learn to fight like that? I reckon you'd call stopping a fight, the way you did, the same thing as fighting."

"Not quite same as fighting," Dorje Lama said, but he was not disturbed by Jebby's perplexity over how a man of peace could give the wrong impression. His serene expression did not change as he explained, "Buddhist Lamas do not seek fights, but defend selves against bandits. In old days, Chinese Lamas walk from China to Tibet. They visit temples and shrines. Sometimes bandit come from behind on lonely roads. He want lama's rice bowl, sometimes lined with silver. He want lama's prayer beads." He pulled out a string of wooden beads from his pocket.

"Lama fight only in self-defense," the Buddhist stranger said. Jebby's eyes widened. He didn't quite understand about the beads and the rice bowls lined with silver, but he did know that the quiet little man was a brave man. He would walk into the midst of battle unafraid, of this Jebby was certain.

"Buddhist lamas of my country learn this special, very ancient way of self-defense from Chinese. It called 'Shao-lin' in China. Five different kinds of 'Shao-lin.' My kind called 'K'ung-chia Shao-lin.'" It come from Honan Province, where run great Yellow River. Buddhist priests bring it to my people not far away. Gegen Abbott in temple taught me 'K'ung-chia Shao-lin' when I was small boy." He stretched out his hand to measure an imaginary boy about four feet tall."

"Just self-defense?" asked Jebby.

Dorje Lama nodded his head. And then and there Jebby resolved to learn to defend himself by this easy-looking method. "Could you teach me?" he asked the Lama.

"Before young boy learn 'K'ung-chia Shao-lin,' he must learn many other things. He must have strong spirit. Teacher must have strong spirit. And lama-teacher spirit-very weak."

Dorje Lama pointed to his heart. 'Lama need calm in here. Today lama weak in here."

"Do you have heart trouble?" Jebby asked.

"No, lad," Major MacFae interjected. "He means weak in the spirit."

"Lama live in small room in big, big house with many people," Dorje Lama explained. "Push button for light. Push button for air—hot air, cold air. Push buttons for box to go up in sky. Many noises—radio, telephone, television. Lama cannot think. Lama cannot say prayers. Lama cannot study the golden path. Lama spirit not calm. Lama spirit grow weak."

Now Jebby understood. Life in Washington was different for him, too. On the farm he never had to bother with self-service elevators. Boxes going into the sky was the way the Lama expressed it. No traffic lights there and no apartment houses.

"I come here to help big American government. It helped me when big political troubles come to Tibet, China, and Mongolia. But now they put me in house too big, too many people. Lama need air, a quiet place. Then he teach young boy."

"Will you tell me about the wild horse, too?" Jebby asked eagerly. Unexpectedly, he snapped his fingers. He had it! A swell idea. "A tent, that's what you need, a little pup tent in the forest. You could be quiet there," he declared.

Major MacFae chuckled and took up the idea. "A pup tent is too small. Tents are hot and stuffy. I have another suggestion. Dorje Lama needs a yurt.... He has lived many a year in Mongolia and I think it will help him."

"What's that, sir?" Jebby asked.

"It's a kind of tent, but the cover is made of felt and stretched over a frame made of willow boughs. They are all over Mongolia. The natives call them a gerr, but Europeans and Americans, for some reason, call them yurts."

He could have gone on to describe how all across Mongolia to the Siberian border, people lived in yurts.

"They are different from wigwams of the American Indians," he explained. "They have a framework made of willow branches. Over this a covering of felt is spread. In summer, the sides can be rolled up. When they are pulled down in winter, the heat is kept inside and it is right cozy. A hole in the center serves as a chimney for the smoke from the cooking fire to escape."

Jebby got the picture.

"We will build you a yurt, Dorje Lama," Major MacFae said. "Look at this lad here—a strong one, all right. He held off that ruffian until Dorje Lama arrived. He will be a great help."

Jebby wondered what would have happened if Dorje Lama hadn't arrived. He reckoned he could indirectly thank the wild mare for that. Major MacFae had said that the Lama would tell him about these horses. No one had ever called him strong before because he was small for his age and everyone judged a boy by his height. But he knew he was strong, even if he wasn't very tall.

The Lama stood there impassive, except for a tiny light of pleasure in his bright black eyes.

"That would be fun," said Jebby. "We could build one of those all right." He liked to build things and use his hands. He was anx-

ious to find a peaceful place for Dorje Lama for the Lama's sake—
and for his own, too, because then he could learn that special kind
of self-defense.

"First, we will have to find a good site," Major MacFae said.

Jebby knew the idea had been accepted.

Dorje Lama spoke. "Yurt will make Lama strong in spirit and
then can teach young boy 'Shao-lin' and tell him about the wild
horse."

These were welcome words to Jebby. "I think we can find a
place somewhere in Rock Creek Park," he said. "It's such a big
park, so many hidden places, tall trees, bushes, hills and valleys.
Golly, Major MacFae and Mr. Lama, I know we can find you a
place."

The Scotsman looked inquiringly at Dorje Lama, who nodded
his head in agreement.

"Well, let's not stand here," the Major said with military brisk-
ness. "Let's go."

5
Search for a Site

Long before European explorers set foot on the shores of the New World, Algonquin Indians of the Powhatan Confederacy roamed the hills and valley that people know today as Rock Creek Park. It was in this beautiful, sometimes rugged, historic place—today rich with spring—that Jebby, Major MacFae and Dorje Lama searched for a hidden site for the Lama's yurt.

Indians once stalked many kinds of animals, such as bear, buffalo elk, bobcat, white-tailed deer, through the creek valley and into the upland forest, taking what they needed for food and clothing and leaving the rest.

As time wore on and men gathered into settlements, a capital city for a new nation was created on the banks of the Potomac. And new statesmen and their families discovered this wondrous place, so bursting in spring with beauty they could hardly describe it. Some tried, though. One of them was a President of the United States. John Quincy Adams once wrote of how he would go into "this romantic glen, listening to the singing of a thousand birds," to forget the cares of office.

So, to help other men set free their cares and to give young people a place that was wild and unspoiled, the Congress of the United States, in 1890, started setting aside nearly 2,000 acres in the heart of the capital. This made Washington a capital city unique in the entire world and beloved by all who knew her.

Even though Jebby was homesick for the ranges of Shenandoah, he felt there was something special, something pretty wonderful about Rock Creek Park. He was beginning to feel like many before him, whether statesmen, Scouts, ambassadors or poets, had felt as they wandered throughout the years down the valleys and up the cliffs. And they could range ten miles in one direction and two miles in another.

But now civilization was pressing closer and roads wound through the park. Even so, Jebby already knew that many animals still called it home. A tiny chipmunk had just scampered by. Above their heads, squirrels chattered, and Jebby knew that, throughout the woods, he could find almost every kind of bird he used to find at home—from common grackles to oven birds. Most of them stayed in the more rugged areas of the Park. And it was in one of these places, among the towering tulip trees, oaks and protective undergrowth, that Jebby and his new friends hoped they could find a site.

The trio followed the path along the stream called Rock Creek for the boulders and rocks that in places almost blocked the waters flowing from their source thirty miles up in Maryland. They passed under cliffs so sheer that Washington boys have looked upon them with the same sense of challenge that Sir Edmund Hillary and Tensing Norkay felt when looking at Mount Everest.

Jebby didn't know it as he walked beneath them, but these cliffs were all that were left of a mountain range that had once covered the entire area of Virginia and Maryland. Some of the peaks rose four miles into the sky one billion years ago. But through the ages streams rushing to the sea had worn them down and turned them into cliffs that, in later years, the Indians found useful. From the quartz and granite they had fashioned tomahawks, arrows and spearheads, and from deposits of soap-stone they had made cooking utensils. In other places in today's park, they had found clays for the extraction of dyes to use in decorating and painting their skin.

Jebby and his two companions today were treading in the moccasin-steps of the braves and hunters of three hundred years ago, who had come to this place from as far away as the Rappahannock. Fortunately, their needs were not so great as those of the Indians who were far from their tribal settlements. They could pass the yellow poplar trees without thinking of felling them to hollow out canoes. And they could see the white ash trees and not invision a smooth-bladed paddle to dip into the waters of the Potomac. But just like their Indian forerunners, Jebby, Major MacFae and Dorje Lama needed a place for their shelter—whether called a wigwam, tent or yurt.

They felt a sense of urgency, even emergency, as they hiked along the stream path on the first stage of their journey to the deep woodland. There they might find a secluded place where no one would find their yurt. Ahead now lay a picnic ground, an old stone mill and then the deep upland forest.

As they passed Peirce Mill, they noticed the miller leaning against the stone wall next to the ancient wheel that was being turned by the waters of the creek. His face and clothes were powdered white. He was smoking his pipe and soaking up the springtime afternoon sun.

"Howdy," he said as the three passed him.

Major MacFae saluted briskly and replied, "Good afternoon." Jebby said, "Hello," and Dorje Lama said, "Mendi, Mendi" and placed his hands together in the Buddhist greeting. They were in such a hurry they didn't wait to notice if the miller was surprised to see such an oddly assorted trio tramping along, headed for the forest.

The creek's surface on the other side of the mill's waterfall was slick as a mirror, and on it glided dozens of white Peking ducks. Mixed in with them were a few glossy green-black mallards that no longer answered the call of the wild.

Along the banks of the stream grew towering, majestic beech trees. The silvery bark of most of them was scarred by carvings of entwined hearts and the initials of lovers of days gone by. And the busy sapsuckers and other woodpeckers had left their marks,

A path that led eventually to a high plateau in the hills
seemed to all three a logical choice to follow . . .

too, in the form of tiny holes drilled by their beaks with relentless efficiency while searching for ants and other insects.

Gentle, sorrowful coos of mourning doves added to the soothing mood of the spring afternoon. It was an hour to pause by the stream and watch the waters bounce and slide over the rocks or to watch a fat queen mother wasp, fresh from hibernation, ready herself for tasks ahead. Jebby felt that to linger just a moment and maybe, even, to stretch out on the banks would be fun. Then he looked at the Major's stern profile and banished the thought. He brought his lagging steps forward and made his stride as purposeful as his companions'. The three must be off now from this lazy scene beside the creek and start the climb to the upland forest.

A path that led eventually to a high plateau in the hills seemed to all three a logical choice to follow when a crossroads offered them a choice. Each of them had a home in the highlands, although of a different land—Scotland, Shenandoah County of Virginia and Central Asia's snow-capped ranges.

At the entrance to the upland trail they came upon a signpost with the head of a black horse painted on it. The low road carried a similar sign, but its horse's head was white.

As the explorers pressed upward on Black Horse Trail, they found the vegetation different from that along the stream. Here, swollen dogwood buds were full of the promise of waxen white blossoms. On the forest floor grew May apple plants with large, wide, scalloped leaves, like so many umbrellas sheltering the round white blossoms, then the fruit, that soon would grow beneath them.

The little chirpy call of the Carolina wren that Jebby thought sounded like "Tea Kettle, Tea Kettle" was mixed in with the incessant calls of the cardinals and mockingbirds.

As they hiked up the path, Major MacFae suddenly stooped down to examine a white wildflower.

"Reminded me there for a moment of a little bloom near the Edsin Gol region. Mongols sometimes say it's good for a horse's wind." He didn't pause as he talked but walked straight on up the path. "Jolly interesting, though. Wonder what it is? Don't know all your blossoms here, yet."

This set Jebby to wondering. Maybe he should be thinking about some new things for Isabella to eat, now that Major MacFae had fed her all of his special steppe grass.

Suddenly, Jebby remembered he hadn't told Major MacFae he had named the mare Isabella. All the excitement over grass and her reunion with her ancestors and the Caps coming and Dorje Lama—well, it was easy to see how he could forget.

"I named the mare Isabella," he announced simply.

Puzzled, Major MacFae looked at him questioningly. Then a light of recollection broke across his face. "Ah, now I remember! I told you that these Isabella-colored horses are killers. Aye, and that they are."

"So now the lad," he was looking at Dorje Lama, "goes out and names the mare Isabella."

"It is a funny name for a color," Jebby said, "but I think it is a pretty name, too—even if you say she's a killer."

"Yes, that name is an old one, started back in the days of Queen Elizabeth and then the Germans borrowed it. It stands for a yellowish-reddish color. These horses are the same color as the wasteland in western Mongolia. Protective coloring, they call it. Many animals have protective coloring—it's their best defense."

"Look at the fawn—its dapples blend in with the leaves and sunlight," Jebby volunteered. Just then, he noticed another white flower alongside the path and bent over to look at it closely. And as he did so, he saw through the trees to his right an opening that seemed to lead to a dell.

"Look, Major MacFae," Jebby called and turned into the forest.

The two men followed the boy through the underbrush leading to a small opening in the trees. When they arrived there, they found that the ground dropped off into a little basin-shaped area. It was cozy and secluded. This, all of them knew right away, was the spot they sought. But none of them said a word. This looked too good to be true!

Dorje Lama's black eyes darted about the little dell. He walked to the edge of the clearing and pointed out a small spring. The water looked cool and fresh. Around it bloomed starlike white flowers on a plant called bloodroot. Its blood-red juice could once have served as war paint for the braves of Chief Powhatan.

"Sain, Sain" the Lama said approvingly. He slipped into his native Kalmuck tongue when he was enthusiastic. And, for once, he smiled broadly.

The Major hurried over to the spring. "A good water supply for our tea." He caught himself. "I mean your tea, Dorje Lama. This is to be your yurt."

The lama smiled again and spoke once more in Kalmuck. "Ta-nai talal yamer baine."

"Sain, sain," said Major MacFae. And then continued in English, "I am glad, very glad that you are happy with this place." Then he said, half to himself, "Ah, for a cup of tea!"

All of this talk about tea, yet Jebby could see no sign of kettle, teacups or a fire to heat the water. But since meeting Major Mac-Fae on the ground yesterday (a thousand years ago, it seemed), nothing surprised him anymore.

The three of them sat on a decayed log to rest after the long, brisk walk. Their secret place was ringed with wild pink azalea bushes.

"Everything is first rate," the Major said, "but no willows, so how will we make the yurt?" He glanced about him for branches of trees that looked supple enough to build the yurt frame. "I thought we might find the short-leaf variety up here."

They examined the trees all around. There were Virginia pine, tulip trees, all kinds of oak and red maple—but no willows!

When they sat again on the log, taking stock of their situation and wondering what to use instead, Jebby watched some large black carpenter ants in the sawdust of the decaying wood. How busy they were—running back and forth, about their little duties! As his thoughts wandered, he began to picture the sawmill in the woods near his grandmother's. He had always hated the spooky whine of those saws.

Then, suddenly, an idea dawned. "I've got it!" he cried, snapping his fingers once more. "The very thing!"

"What's that?" The Major looked up, interested in what the boy had to offer.

"Molding strips. They'll do it. You can get them at most hardware stores. They'll bend just fine and make a good frame for the yurt. They used to make them at a sawmill near us. And, hey, there's a hardware store on the avenue and we can take a short cut there and won't even have to go back through the Zoo."

Major MacFae rose to his feet. The Lama rose, too. The three of them headed through the woods and followed the path that would take them to the road leading to the hardware store. There, they were sure, they would find the basic materials for building the yurt.

6

In Xanadu

Jebby did not find it easy to keep his mind on what his English teacher, Miss Pepper, was saying.

He was thinking, instead, of the trip to the hardware store yesterday afternoon, where they had bought aluminum strips for the yurt frame. The wood molding strips would have served very well, but when Dorje Lama had spied the silvery, yet willowy-looking, strips—they were do-it-yourself poles—he had decided, then and there, that an aluminum frame was what he wanted for his yurt.

Major MacFae had suggested that the aluminum strips be hidden in the woods near the Zoo, instead of taking them back to their secret place in Rock Creek Park. He had been very insistent on that. He instructed Jebby to come straight to the yurt site when school was out because they would need him in putting up the center ring. This was the top of the frame where smoke could get out.

Jebby hoped he could get down to the secret place without being seen by the Caps. Shad and Bo were scared stiff yesterday after Dorje Lama and Major MacFae finished with them; but, if they caught him out loose without his protectors—well, he didn't like to think of all of them piling on him. He must learn soon from the Lama how to defend himself.

Jebby's daydreaming stopped when he realized suddenly that Miss Pepper was talking about the Zoo. He turned his head from the window and looked at her. She was speaking earnestly, and her face was bright with enthusiasm. Jebby liked her, for she made everything come so alive.

She held a leaflet in her hand now. "Let me repeat the announcement," she said. "The Friends of the Zoo are holding a contest for the best essay on the general subject of 'A trip into literature, science or history with my favorite Zoo animal.' The winner of the essay contest will be given a life membership in the Friends of the Zoo." She paused and looked up from the announcement sheet before continuing. "The nicest part of the contest, I think, is permitting the winner to give a name to the next baby animal born at the Zoo. He or she can name it for himself or for herself, as the case may be," Miss Pepper explained. "But I imagine you would rather name it for a friend or somebody in your family."

Jebby was thinking about Isabella. Surely, there was no animal in the Zoo more important scientifically and historically than the wild mare—the horse he would tame and ride someday. But about literature on the subject, he did not know. Had anyone ever written a book about the true wild horses, he wondered.

"It can be a straight factual essay or you can bring in references to or quotations from poetry or famous books about certain animals, birds or fish," Miss Pepper continued. As she spoke, Katie Peterson's hand went up. She had long blonde hair, worn in a pony-tail, and gray, thoughtful eyes. Jebby had talked to her a few times and thought she was nice. Pretty, too.

"Miss Pepper," she asked, "I could write about the albatross, couldn't I? There's one at the Zoo. And then I could tell all about the albatross in the poem, The Ancient Mariner. We live so far from the ocean that we never see sea birds out in Wyoming. My father is in Congress."

"The albatross brought the Ancient Mariner bad luck, Katie," Miss Pepper reminded her.

"Yes, but only because the Ancient Mariner, when he was a young man, shot him. He was sorry later—truly sorry. He was guiding the ship and really helping the sailors. 'With my cross bow I shot the albatross,'" Katie said. She had a triumphant look on her face for having remembered that line of the poem.

"Do you know the rest?" Miss Pepper asked.

"No, not exactly; but the poem is trying to tell you not to go about killing innocent birds and animals," Katie replied.

"How many of you know the poem?" Miss Pepper asked.

Only a few hands were raised.

"Well," Miss Pepper said, picking up her literature book, "after the sailor shot the bird, the wind stopped blowing and the ship was becalmed. It had only sails. There were no motors in those days. I am sure that you have all heard these lines." She read:

"Water, water everywhere
And all the boards did shrink
Water, water everywhere
Nor any drop to drink."

"The dying crew," Miss Pepper continued, "hung the dead albatross around the sailor's neck. So that's where you get the expression—'an albatross around my neck.' The sailor watched them die. And then they turned into ghosts that tormented him. Finally, the ship came to shore. And the sailor was doomed to wander forever, asking people not to harm birds and animals. When he was an old man, he told people:

'He prayeth best, who loveth best
All things both great and small;
For the dear God who loveth us,
He made and loveth all.'"

Jebby liked these words—they said what he felt.

Miss Pepper had scarcely finished reading the lines when Bo's hand shot up. "Did you say we could write about animals in science—animals they have at the Zoo?" he asked.

"Certainly," replied Miss Pepper.

"Well, then I want to write my essay about the first monkey in space," Bo said.

The boy next to him, "You can't just write about one monkey. There were two that went up at the same time. Their names were Able and Baker. It was long ago, way back in 1959, I think. The first astronaut didn't come until two years later."

Before the boy could finish, other hands shot up and a boy in the back volunteered, "I want to write about Smokey the Bear."

"I think I'll pick the elephant," said another.

"How about Rudolph, the Red Nosed Reindeer?" Lucky snickered.

The class was becoming enthusiastic. The only two students who had not raised their hands were Shad and Jebby.

Miss Pepper looked at the sullen Shad and called on him, trying to make him take part with the others.

"How about you, Shad?"

He shook his head, then, after a pause, grunted, "Tiger."

Miss Pepper replied, "Good, I have the very thing, Shad!" She began to read again:

"Tiger, tiger burning bright
In the forest of the night,
What immortal hand or eye
Framed thy fearful symmetry?

"What the hammer? What the chain?
In what furnace was thy brain?
What the anvil? What dread grasp,
Dared its deadly terrors clasp?"

Shad looked more interested the more Miss Pepper read. When she finished, the big, gangling boy, the chief tough of Winston Junior High, leaned over to his pal, Bo. "That's me—the tiger."

As soon as he said this, Katie Peterson's hand went up again. "Miss Pepper," she said, "there's another verse of that poem. I think Shad should hear it, since he thinks he's such a tiger." The girl smiled mischievously, then began to recite in a clear, high voice:

"When the stars threw down their spears
And watered heaven with their tears,
Did He smile His work to see?
Did He who made the lamb make thee?"

Shad scowled as she read. Comparing him with a lamb was an insult! His classmates grinned, some tittered. So with that, Shad rose and headed out of the classroom.

"The class has not been dismissed," Miss Pepper said briskly. "Take your seat, Shad." There was a command in her voice. The tiger, lamblike, took his seat.

Miss Pepper did not want to embarrass him further, so she quickly turned to Jebby, who, up until now, had not taken part in the discussion. "Have you made your selection?"

"Yes, ma'am," Jebby replied. He wanted to tell, yet this horse was his secret.

"It's a horse—"

Bo laughed, and Shad joined him. "He can't think of anything better than a horse," Bo said.

Jebby could feel his neck redden as anger rose inside him.

"This horse is different," he told Miss Pepper. He tried to ignore Bo's whispers.

"In what way?" his teacher asked.

He didn't want to answer that question—for he didn't know all about the wild mare yet. They were pushing him for details, but all he was going to say now was that she was unusual. He would save the reasons why for his essay.

"Just—just different," he replied.

Again Shad interrupted the class. "She don't look like the horses out in the sticks." He was obviously referring to Jebby being a new boy from the country.

Jebby's anger rose higher and higher and he clenched his fists.

"Maybe she's first cousin to a jackass," Bo said, tormenting him.

Miss Pepper rapped for attention but Jebby could stand the teasing no longer. The words came tumbling out. "She's different because she's the true wild horse," he shouted. "She was living when cave men were living. She's so wild that even Mongolians can't ride her."

"Mongolians?" the teacher repeated questioningly.

"Yes, ma'am." Jebby's anger subsided, now that the class knew he was planning to write about the wild horse. "Genghis Khan couldn't even handle these horses," Jebby said proudly.

Miss Pepper looked even more surprised. She flipped the pages in her literature book. "That gives me an idea," she said. "Listen:

'In Xanadu did Kubla Khan
A stately pleasure-dome decree:
Where Alph, the sacred river, ran
Through caverns measureless to man
Down to a sunless sea.'

"Kubla Khan was Genghis' son or grandson," Miss Pepper explained.

Jebby listened intently. That line about the caverns was interesting because Major MacFae had talked about the wild horses' pictures being painted on the walls of caves.

Miss Pepper continued reading:

"And here were forests as ancient as the hills
Enfolding sunny spots of greenery.
But Oh! that deep romantic chasm which slanted
Down the green hill athwart a cedarn cover
A savage place!"

Jebby sat there dumfounded—caves and romantic chasms slanting down a green hill. It was almost as if the poet had been looking over his shoulder for the last two days.

"Miss Pepper," he asked, "what was the name of that poem?"

"Kubla Khan," she replied.

The English teacher looked at Jebby and then Katie. "Did you know that Kubla Khan and The Ancient Mariner were written by the same poet?" she asked. "His name was Samuel Taylor Coleridge."

The bell almost drowned out her words, "And he was a true romantic."

But Jebby and Katie heard her and smiled at each other. A bond was being established between them, even in the midst of the noise of class changing, the scraping of chairs being pushed back, shuffling feet and the hubbub of chattering voices.

As the two walked down the corridor together, Jebby, on impulse, was on the verge of sharing with this understanding girl his secret dream to take Isabella away from the bare paddock she hated to free green pastures. He might even tell Katie that one day he would ride the wild mare.

That seemingly natural walk of Jebby and Katie, down the hall to their next class was to prove a more important walk than either of them realized then. They were just a boy and girl who wanted to get on with the job of going to school but Jebby had found that, if he wasn't careful, more time could be spent fighting a rearguard action than learning anything. At least, that was the way Winston Junior High was working out.

Before Jebby could confide in Katie, however, Shad and Bo passed them. Shad muttered something under his breath about, "You'd better not let me catch you alone."

Then Bo said to Shad loudly, pretending Jebby wasn't even there, "You know that kid is always hiding behind somebody's skirts. First it's that old Scotch fellow and now it's Katie Peterson."

Jebby's face turned red. That was a lie! He was only talking to the girl, not hiding behind her skirts—or Major MacFae's either. He turned to grab Bo, who swaggered on down the hall, but Katie put her hand on his arm.

"Don't do it, Jebby. That's what they want you to do. They want a big fight here at school so they can gang up on you in front of everybody—even if they get demerits or kicked out for it. They don't care what happens to them. Their families don't even care. Nobody knows anything at all about Shad's mother and dad. He lives with a sister or somebody. And he has nobody to hold him down or care whether he gets kicked out. But you don't want to get kicked out with him."

Just like Major MacFae, this girl, Jebby thought, was full of caution. The Scotsman had said they should use their heads instead of their fists. But headwork doesn't do much good when a fellow slugs you, except to duck. You have to learn to protect yourself. And that was exactly what he was going to do. Two more hours of school and he could go to the secret place and get his first lesson from Dorje Lama.

"Don't worry about me," Jebby told Katie with a grin. But inside he didn't mind her solicitude—at all!

7
Building the Yurt

He made it!

After that quarrel in the hall, Jebby was sure the Caps would tail him when he left school for the day. But he used a side door and took a back route to his apartment house. He had preferred to go straight to the yurt so he could get his first "Shao-lin" lesson from Dorje Lama, but he had promised to bring his friend the rose-design hooked rug that Grandmother had made. When he had described it, Major MacFae had said it would do fine as a door to the yurt.

So now, with the rug under his arm, Jebby was heading toward Black Horse Trail. He was taking a different course, by-passing the Zoo where the Caps might be lying in wait. Even though he was hurrying, he noticed that the April warmth was bringing out many little wildflowers. He passed tiny, delicate white spring beauties, a jack-in-the-pulpit and box elder bushes. If there had been more time, he would have lingered to make a whistle out of the box elder stems. But Xanadu could not wait. The building of the yurt could not wait. The lesson from Dorje Lama could not wait. And he could not wait to tell his new friends the news about the essay contest and that he planned to write about Isabella.

At last! There was the sign of the Black Horse Trail. In about three more minutes he would reach the dell. That fresh spring water would taste good.

It was a secret place indeed. For a moment Jebby couldn't find it himself. He remembered that he must look for a rotten horn-beam log. Then he went six paces farther and turned into the deep wood.

He pushed aside the wild azalea bushes. And there they were. The dell was transformed! Rich Oriental rugs were spread over the ground and a brass pot was hanging over a small fire in a charcoal stove. Dorje Lama and Major MacFae were sitting cross-legged on a dark red rug with the blue and yellow designs. They were inserting screws in the end of the aluminum poles and had made a very presentable looking lattice to serve as a frame for Dorje Lama's yurt.

"Put your rug over there, lad." Major MacFae indicated a pile of rugs under the pine tree on his right.

"Now, Jebby, there's work for you. Take these pieces here." He handed him two aluminum strips. "See this screw, it's what they call a self-tapping screw. Very clever. You don't have to have a nut to hold it. Smashing good idea." It was clear that the Major approved.

Jebby held the crossed pieces of aluminum, as the Major inserted the screw to hold them together.

Jebby was puzzled by the big pile of assorted material, the charcoal stove and the brass pot. "How did you bring all of this stuff down to the yurt? How many trips did you take? I could have helped you."

"Only one trip," the Major answered.

"Oh, no!" Jebby groaned. "Not one trip?"

"Our load didn't weigh more than five hundred pounds, did it, Dorje Lama?" the old Scotsman remarked with a twinkle in his bright blue eyes.

Dorje Lama nodded in agreement. His face betrayed nothing.

"Five hundred pounds! But you couldn't have carried all that unless you made several trips. I could have helped you, Major. I wanted to, but you said I should go home. Who helped you, sir?"

"An old friend," he replied and then began to recite:

"Fair fa' your honest sousie face."

"Haggis!" exclaimed Jebby. "Haggis!"

"Aye, you guessed it, lad. Her humps are not so good, but the old girl did very well," the Major declared with a chuckle. "Besides, this was an emergency. Our Lama here needs a quiet place, eh son?"

You came down here at night and no one saw you? And no one missed the old camel from her pen?" Jebby asked. It must have been fun."

"Yes, it was rather jolly," the Major remarked in an offhand way. "Haggis liked it, too."

For a few minutes Jebby worked diligently on the lattice frame, but his thoughts were with Isabella. Maybe he could bring her out of the pen under the cover of darkness and try to ride her.

"Do you think I could—"

The Major didn't let him finish his sentence. "Now, laddie, I've warned you about the mare. So no ideas now. Besides, her paddock is well locked."

"Well, then, sir," Jebby asked with mounting curiosity, "How did you get old Haggis out?"

"Ah, you'd never believe it, Andrews. That you'd not. But her wooden gate was so rotten that the hasp that held the lock almost fell in my hands when I touched it. So, laddie, you might say, I just opened the gate and walked in and borrowed the old girl for a few hours."

"Golly!" was all Jebby could say.

"Took her right into the forest, loaded her and set off. You see, lad, they use another gate, those keepers do. That old gate hasn't been used in years. But as I told you," and the Major raised a warning hand, "no ideas, now. D'ye hear me, laddie? The mare's not for riding. Dorje Lama can tell you that."

"Major speaks the truth," the Lama said. "Mongolian wild mare dangerous. Horse is killer."

"Did you ever try, Dorje Lama?" Jebby asked.

A look of positive fright swept across the Lama's usually serene face. "Never! Too dangerous."

"Well, I wish somebody would explain to me about these horses."

Major MacFae looked at the Lama as if to give him the signal to tell Jebby all he knew.

"I am a Kalmuck," Dorje Lama said. "My people travel much in Tibet, in Mongolia, China and Siberia. My people know the tiger, the goat, the camel. They do not fear them. But my people fear wild horse."

"But why?" Jebby insisted.

"Wild horse no good to man. He stomp man to the ground. Break his bones. Then small dragon come and finish the killing."

Jebby was puzzled by this reference to a dragon but the Lama went right ahead with his explanation. "Horse live in far distant secret lands where mountains meet. Four tribes live in Dzungaria, which is near Russia and China. My people live there, but leave wild horse in peace. We know about horse many years but say nothing. One day, big Russian explorer, like Major MacFae, come to our land. His name was Colonel Nicholas Przewalski. He was looking for wild camels. Instead, hunters bring him one of wild horses. It is dead. He looked at it and think it is one ancestor of horse. Very important discovery."

Major MacFae broke in to explain, "That's why it's called Przewalski's horse."

"He never saw it alive?" Jebby asked.

"No, never. The skeleton is in Russia now, in a Museum. Leningrad, I believe."

"Big news finding true wild horse," the Lama said. "Zoo men in Europe want to find live wild horses, too. Big business to show wild horse to world. Make much money."

"But it was more than money," the Major broke in. "Finding this stone age horse is to the world of animals what finding a live stone age man would be to the world of modern man."

"No kidding," said Jebby. It was almost too much to take in.

"Yes, Andrews, I do mean it. These horses are living fossils.

So those roundups back there at the turn of the century were the most important wild horse roundups ever held in the world. The only true wild horse roundups, I should say."

"Were the horses hard to catch?" Jebby asked.

"Dreadfully hard. I wish I knew all the details. Fact and legend have become mixed together. But anyway, these Europeans—Germans and Russians—who masterminded the roundups had to make preparations for almost a whole year. They had to travel through the most desolate country of Central Asia even to get close to the breeding area. Then they had to wait for the colts to be born. They knew it would be easier to catch the young ones."

Dorje Lama then took up the story. "Men wait for colts to get bigger. Then they get together many Kalmuck men on horseback for big wild-horse hunt. I hear story from old Kalmuck men at place called Kobdo. Now I tell you all I hear."

This was almost like an eyewitness description, Jebby thought, as he sat there cross-legged, chin cupped in his hands on the rich red rug from the fabulous world of the Far East.

"When colts and mothers come to river to drink," Dorje Lama began, "men on horseback start chase and follow wild horses. But young colts and mothers at first run very fast. Men chase wild horses for miles and miles across the steppes. Horses very strong. Do not get tired. But men and horses chasing them grow very tired. New horses and new men take up chase."

Major MacFae explained. "He means that fresh horses and riders were stationed throughout the large area, like relays, going after the poor beasts. Amazing stamina!"

"That doesn't seem fair, does it?" Jebby questioned. He could picture the herd of horses with their colts running frantically across the plains of this far distant land, with the relentless men behind them.

"Chasing men scream at wild horses. These unhappy horses do not like loud screaming noises. This frightens them. Horses follow close, one after other," Dorje Lama added.

"He means single file," the Major interpreted.

"Hunters scream very loud—they come to get colts

that are left behind. But stallion tries to stomp them."

"Colts grow tired and mothers try to stay with them, but stallion he make them go ahead with others. He go and shove colts with his nose. He bite colts, he pull them, he push them. Stallion very good father. Hunters scream very, very loud—they come to get colts that are left behind. But stallion comes and tries to stomp them. He knock one rider off horse. He kill him. Small dragon come and sting rider lying in sand."

"Small dragon?" Jebby managed to voice his amazement this time.

Major MacFae hastened to explain. "It is a kind of deadly poisonous snake found out there—the Kalmucks are terribly afraid of it. It is called Ologor horhai—that means pot snake. They put it in a cooking pot because they are afraid to kill it. They even feed it so it will stay alive in there."

"Why?"

Dorje Lama, listening closely, replied. "When he die, something happen to man. Man fall over and die."

Jebby whistled—a long, low whistle, then asked, "Do they have one here at the Zoo reptile house?"

Dorje Lama shook his head.

"No," Major MacFae replied. "I must admit I've never seen one. I never heard this part of round up story but Mongolia is full of tales of dragons and spirits."

"What else does the wild stallion do?" Jebby questioned.

"He fight and fight. But he cannot win and then one hunter take gun and shoot wild stallion. Then hunter come and take young colts. Colts fight, too. So men tie legs and drag them away. They leave their mothers."

Jebby had a mental picture of the scene—the little colts and fillies, their bodies covered by foaming sweat, their sides heaving, their young hearts bursting from the long run, and panic in their eyes from being jerked away from their mothers—their source of milk.

"How did these hunters feed these foals?" Jebby asked.

"They give them to mares—regular horses—they brought with

them. They had young colts and had milk in their breasts. But hunters kill mares' own colts and put wild colts in place to raise."

"That's awful!" Jebby cried indignantly. "Poor little colts—both kinds, the dead ones and the live ones!"

"Maybe that is another reason why Isabella doesn't like people very much," Major MacFae declared. "Genetic memory, as I told you, lad. Somehow she inherited the remembrance of how cruel men were to her grandparents. Cave men chased them and ate them—but never rode them. And then, when these wild horses thought they had a quiet place in which to live, far, far away from man, years later hunters come great distance to bring them out. Ruddy shame! But you can see why we don't want you to try and get on Isabella's back. She might trample you."

Before Jebby could say anything, Major MacFae was on his feet, picking up the light aluminum frame. "Give me a hand, there, will you?" he asked.

The boy scrambled to his feet and held one end of the lattice section.

"We fasten this piece here," said the Major, "and there.... Good, she's coming along fine!"

They put the circular frame in place on the ground and it seemed to look just right. Next, the strips that would support the semi-slated roof had to be connected with the frame. The self-tapping screws did that very well.

"Now the whole idea, Andrews, is to attach one end of these strips to the frame we have standing here and the other end to the circle up in the air. You see, these strips are not as flexible as the others. They will hold firmly up in the air the small circle that will serve as a smoke vent. We wouldn't be able to fit those roof rods into the hoop if we didn't have you to do it. Now, you'll have to sit on my shoulders. The Lama will fit the other ends into the lattice frame, in the meanwhile."

"O.K.," Jebby agreed. "Hope I am not too heavy for you, sir."

"Too heavy for me," the Major echoed with a snort as he stooped over. "Nonsense!"

Jebby slipped off his shoes to lighten the burden, also to make it easier to climb on the Major's shoulders. He put a foot on each side of the Scotsman's head and Major MacFae, still stooping, held tight to his ankles. Soon the boy was standing erect and Dorje Lama was handing him a rod. It fitted nicely into the slots in the circle.

"Bravo!" exclaimed the Major. His voice sounded strained and muffled from the effort of bending over and holding the boy, all at the same time.

The trio worked very fast and, within a few minutes, the rods were firmly attached to the circle that would be at the top of the yurt.

Jebby promptly jumped down from the Major's shoulders, which were beginning to sag just the slightest bit.

"Now," said the Major, "we must cover the frame with these rugs I brought from the British Embassy. Very handsome."

Jebby wondered if he could possibly have borrowed property that belonged to the British government!

The Major evidently read the boy's thoughts, for he said, "They're mine. Gave them to my son to keep—and what do you think he does with them? Puts them in the storage room."

He walked over to the pile of rugs that had been garnered from many parts of the Near and Far East. There was a white Kashmiri numbda, made of goat's wool that had been soaked in goat's milk, then dried and rolled to make a strong, heavy material. There was a handsome yellow and red Turkestan rug and a fine product of Persia, with geometric designs of blue, pink and yellow. And the handsomest of all was a dark red rug, with rectangular designs. "This is a Royal Bokhara," the Major explained. "We will save it for the floor of the yurt."

The rugs were heavy, so it took combined efforts of the three to drape them around the yurt. Major MacFae made them fast with large safety pins.

Nowhere in Outer Mongolia—that mysterious land of nomadic herdsmen—could there be a handsomer yurt, Jebby decided.

Fit for a king—fit, in this case, for a homesick Lama in Washington, D. C.

"How about calling it Xanadu?" Jebby asked.

Major MacFae looked surprised, then began to declaim in loud tones:

"In Xanadu did Kubla Khan
A stately pleasure-dome decree...."

He slapped the boy on the shoulder. "A fine name, lad!"

"I just learned it today—the poem, I mean," Jebby admitted. "That's what I wanted to tell you—all about the poem and the essay contest." Then he blurted out, "I've just got to have those special lessons in that Lama-kind of defense when attacked. It's because of what happened in English class."

Major MacFae shook his head. "Now, lad, your story is mixed up. Essay, Xanadu, K'ung-chia Shao-lin lesson. Let's get it straight."

"Well, sir, we have to write an essay about our favorite animal in the Zoo. It's a contest. I said I would write about Isabella because she's the true wild horse and nobody could ride her. The Caps began to mock me. They said the horse was tame. But most of all, they acted as if they were going to try again to get me, so I must learn that special way of protecting myself." Jebby's voice was full of urgency. "I just must!" He was almost pleading.

Dorje Lama rose from the Royal Bokhara rug, where he had been resting, and walked over to Jebby. "Stand up," he said. When the boy had obeyed, he commanded, "Push me."

As Jebby moved toward him the Lama grabbed his arm, and, in a flash, the boy was on the ground, flat on his back and breathless.

Jebby sat up and started shaking his head. "That was some throw," he said. "Can you teach me to do that?"

"Not today," Dorje Lama replied. "First you must learn simple rules."

Jebby scrambled to his feet. The Lama said, "Come here, walk to me." When Jebby was close to him, the Lama placed his right index finger horizontally across the boy's upper lip. "Push," he commanded.

Jebby pushed, but he couldn't even take one step forward. He tried to turn his head, but the finger turned with him. He stepped back, but the Lama stepped forward, and the finger still seemed to block him. The only way he felt he could advance would be to try and knock the Lama's hand down. And, of course, that would have been easy enough with a boy his own size, but not the agile Lama. This unusual way of defense, Jebby could plainly see, was to slow down his opponent so he could give himself time to get at the attacker in an even more effective way.

The Lama removed his finger and walked over to where he had neatly placed two sticks side by side. He picked them up and held them in front of him.

"Two sticks," he said.

"First stick is the same as man full of fear," he told Jebby. He bent it and it snapped sharply in two pieces. "Man full of fear has muscles all tense. His body become like brittle stick. If other man bend him, his bones break." Then he held forth the green stick. "If man have no fear in his heart, his muscles relaxed. If bent, man snaps back." He bent the maple branch, released it, and it snapped back.

Jebby had never before thought of man this way—frightened man like the dead stick; brave man like the green stick.

"Many lessons to learn in this art," said the Lama. "You must think on them long time and you have to practice. Control of mind and heart as important as control of body."

"Is it true," Major MacFae asked the Lama, "that you have to yield if you want to conquer?"

"Yes," replied Dorje Lama, "that is why I showed stick. The stick that yields never broken. Make man use his own strength against himself, like stick that snaps back. Many things to learn. Let me show you something else. Try again to knock me down."

Jebby rushed at the Lama, who grabbed his shirt and, at the same time, stuck his foot out and tripped the boy, who went sprawling again.

Jebby jumped up quickly this time. "Let me try it, Dorje Lama," he begged.

"All right, now stand with your weight on your right foot and, as I come at you, grab me and swing your weight with my body and twist hands, so ..."

Jebby tried to follow the instructions, but he couldn't budge the Lama.

We have another lesson tomorrow. Boy learn enough today. Think on what I show you. Now we drink tea?"

The water in the brass pot was now boiling. Major MacFae rummaged in an old musette bag and brought out three blue and white teacups.

"Brought them from the British Embassy," he announced.

"From the storage room?" Jebby laughed.

The three of them sat drinking tea in front of their yurt, tired but happy. The afternoon was cool, the leaves on the trees were yet a young green. It seemed to be a very good world.

"One day, we'll have a feast here at Dorje Lama's yurt, and I'll bring my pipes and play us a highland tune," the Major said.

Yes, the world seemed full of promise to Jebby—perhaps, even promise of taming the killer mare.

8

On Capitol Hill

While Jebby was building the yurt, hearing the story of the wild horse roundup and getting his fist Shao-lin lesson, Katie Peterson was thinking hard. She decided that her friend was in real danger and, if her father had lots of power, the way United States Senators are supposed to have, he was the man to help Jebby. So, at dinner that night, she told her father all about Jebby's troubles and danger from the Caps.

It was this story that Senator Elias Peterson was pondering as he hurried down the halls of the new marble Senate Office Building the next day. He was late, but Senators are so busy that they are not required to arrive exactly on the dot at committee hearings. They can stay just for a few moments or remain the entire time to hear and question witnesses. Often they attend meetings of two committees and take part in Senate debate all in one day. The young Senator had learned early that it is in the committees that most of the Senate's work on bills is done. These bills—if the committees approve them—later come up for debate and a vote in the Senate chamber.

Senator Peterson belonged to one committee that dealt with the country's health and welfare problems and to another committee that regulated the affairs of the nation's capital.

It was a coincidence that the story Katie had told him about Jebby and his problems was the concern of both of these committees. The committee on health and welfare thought a lot about bad boys and why they acted that way. Their gang fights and misdeeds were becoming a national problem, a national sickness, Senator Peterson thought. Having these young people run wild through the National Zoo was unthinkable. They could become wilder than the animals. The poor, imprisoned animals, he believed, have a right to be wild. But how an animal could continue to be a self-respecting wild beast in that dilapidated place baffled him.

It was inexcusable that the National Zoo should be so antiquated that some of the poor animals had to live the life of a criminal from the days of the dark ages in miserable cages. Their only crime was being special representatives of their kind. True, with the food and protection they received in the Zoo they might live longer than they probably would in their native habitats. But to young Senator Peterson, who liked to ride, ski, swim, hike, freedom to move about as he pleased was important. In order to live to a ripe old age, these animals had to sacrifice their freedom. Even so, it should not be a jail.

By now, the tanned and athletic-looking young Senator from Wyoming was slipping into his seat on the raised platform in the walnut-paneled committee room. The chairman of the committee nodded to him in welcome.

A neatly dressed woman with her white hair parted in the middle was sitting in the witness chair, at a table in the center of the room. Her mouth was a prim, straight line, but her dark brown eyes were so gentle that, at first look, anyone could tell that here was someone with love and kindness in her heart. She had been reading aloud from a sheaf of papers in her hand, but she put them down just as Senator Peterson entered the room.

"Thank you, Miss Bell," said the man seated in the middle of the U-shaped raised platform. He was Senator Lester Hillary, chairman of the committee. "Now I am sure the members of our committee would like to ask you questions about your work as director of the Children's Bureau."

The questioning began, and every word spoken was taken

down by a stenotypist on a quiet little machine. In a few weeks, the Senators would have a printed book to read, containing a record of what was said. With this, they could better judge the requests being made of them.

Several of the Senators on the raised platform asked Miss Bell questions. Then Senator Peterson's turn came.

The stenotyped report read like this:

SENATOR PETERSON: Thank you, Mr. Chairman. Miss Bell, I would like to ask you a few questions. How seriously does the Children's Bureau concern itself with juvenile delinquents? We just called them bad boys—and girls — in my day?

MISS BELL: We study all the problems of children from infancy on up to twenty-one years of age. We recommend what we consider the best methods of approach to these problems. We are also undertaking special studies on the reasons for juvenile delinquency and how we can help solve this gigantic problem.

SENATOR PETERSON: The juvenile delinquency rate is increasing steadily, isn't it? Do you have any figures on that?

MISS BELL: It rises each year, sir. Even though our child population increases each year, at the same time a larger proportion is getting into trouble each year. I will put the figures and percentages and other statistics in the record, sir.

SENATOR PETERSON: What is the main offense?

MISS BELL: Destruction of property, gang fights—yokings, both of children of their own age and of adults. We have homicides, too.

SENATOR PETERSON: I have a fourteen-year-old daughter, Miss Bell, and she tells me what's going on at her school. So, you can see I have a personal interest in these problems. Now, just one or two more questions, please. How many of these children are from the cities and how many from rural areas?

MISS BELL: I don't have the exact figures with me, but the greater majority, I'd say about ninety per cent, were from the cities.

SENATOR PETERSON: How do you account for this?

MISS BELL: Children in the country have more running space, more duties. The family is more tightly knit. Housing is better. They are closer to the soil and animals and learn nature's laws early.

SENATOR PETERSON: Until lately I never heard of many farmer's sons getting into trouble. With so much mechanization and the swallowing up of the small farms by the large ones, though, the picture is beginning to change. But my concern is with these city youngsters. We need to give them something more than baseball diamonds and playgrounds. We've got to get some of the farm to them. But how?

MISS BELL: I think for a child to keep busy and to work with animals is one of the greatest guarantees we can have against juvenile deliquency. There is no substitute for nature. We are so pleased with the Audubon Society's Nature Centers for Young America, the Junior Defenders of Wildlife and other such programs, and, of course, what the Boy and Girl Scouts are doing along this line.

SENATOR PETERSON: You think there is a definite need for more of that sort of thing?

MISS BELL: Most definitely, sir.

SENATOR PETERSON: Thank you, Miss Bell. You have been a very helpful witness. Now, Mr. Chairman, since I have another committee meeting at this very moment, may I be excused?

CHAIRMAN: Certainly.

Elias Peterson's mind was clicking as fast as the wheels of the Senate's little subway car were turning. These open electric cars, running on narrow gauge tracks between the Capitol and the Senate Office Buildings, saved the Senators many steps several times a day. The distance was equivalent to nearly two city blocks. Today Senator Peterson's other committee was holding its meeting in the Capitol Building itself. These few moments on the fast little car, with the air beating against his face and blowing his light hair, gave time to think about the hearing he had just left.

Miss Bell's agreement on the need for opportunities for boys and girls to work and live with wildlife was the kind of cooperation he needed if he was to put over the plan that was now taking shape in his mind. Washington, D. C. would become a pilot project for the whole nation, if his plan worked.

When the subway car arrived in the Capitol, he jumped off and hurried to the elevators that would take him to the floor where his appropriations subcommittee was conducting hearings on the budget of this Capital city. As he entered the room, he saw several officials sitting in the audience, waiting their turn to testify. One of them was the director of the National Zoological Park.

The chairman, Senator Robert R. Hurd, nodded as Senator Peterson took his seat. The witness was picking up his papers and returning to his chair in the audience.

The chairman looked at Senator Peterson and then at the Zoo director and said, "I see Senator Peterson has arrived. He is from the great state of Wyoming, where more wildlife abounds than people. I know that he would like to hear about our Zoo needs. Mr. Bush, will you step forward, please, and tell us your problems, sir."

The stenotypist, a slim, sandy-haired man wearing glasses, took down the following testimony:

MR. BUSH: Thank you, sir. I sometimes think I have 2,400 problems.

CHAIRMAN: You mean you have that many birds, snakes and four-footed animals in the National Zoo?

MR. BUSH: Exactly—and more on the way. We have a rather high birth rate at the Zoo. We need a maternity ward to take care of them. But that is only a dream. More important, we don't have enough personnel to guard these animals properly.

CHAIRMAN: Why do you need to guard them? Can they escape?

MR. BUSH: I hope not, sir, but we need them to guard the animals against hoodlums. We have had tennis balls swallowed by elephants. We have had the necks of our swans wrung. And we have had umbrellas poked at the monkeys, severely injuring them.

CHAIRMAN: The last time you were before our committee, you spoke of the old buildings and small paddocks. I was out at the Zoo recently and noticed that one of the buildings was locked and you had a sign "Unsafe" nailed on the door. What did that mean?

MR. BUSH: Some of our buildings are ancient, timbers rotten—and we have to close them to the public.

CHAIRMAN: How old, would you say?

MR. BUSH: The antelope house goes back to the beginning of the twentieth century.

CHAIRMAN: I see Senator Peterson has a question. Go ahead, Senator.

SENATOR PETERSON: Thank you, Mr. Chairman. I wondered if Mr. Bush could give us a brief history of our National Zoo. It does seem strange to me that a National Zoo, which is for the enjoyment of all the people of the nation—just like the Washington Monument—should be supported only by the people who live in Washington. We should let Uncle Sam pay for all of this National Zoo.

CHAIRMAN: Go ahead, Mr.Bush, and tell us briefly how the Zoo got into this fix.

MR. BUSH: I would like to start, if I may, with the background story of the breechloader gun and the American bison—buffalo, most of us call the animal. Well, sir, after the breechloader was invented in the 1880s, American bison nearly faced extinction. It is hard for us to believe it, but man practically went mad—he was trigger happy with his new gun. He shot from horseback, from stagecoach, even from train windows, as he traveled across the great plains. Do you know, sir, they tell the story that so many bison were killed that a man could jump from carcass to carcass for fifty miles without touching the ground? Sometimes these vandals just shot them for their tongues to eat and their tails to use as fly swatters!

CHAIRMAN: No, I did not know all this, sir.

MR. BUSH: This brings me to the point of my story. There were only about one thousand buffalo left, here and in Canada, by 1889, according to Mr. William Hornaday, who had headed the Department of Living Animals at the

Smithsonian Institution.

SENATOR PETERSON: So, establishing a National Zoo to preserve some of these animals became necessary?

MR. BUSH: It did two things. Gave the Smithsonian downtown a place for its living animals and offered a haven for those species that were being hunted down. Interesting thing, among the first animals presented to the Zoo were three American elk from the famous "Buffalo Bill" Cody.

SENATOR PETERSON: Why wasn't the Zoo established as a government institution, like our national parks and monuments?

MR. BUSH: That was what was intended. But, to beg your pardon, sir, some members of Congress in those days thought a zoo was frivolous, so they voted it down. Finally, it was tacked onto a city budget bill, which was passed. Of course, it is directed by the Smithsonian Institution.

SENATOR PETERSON: You have done a very good job under trying conditions. You have rare animals from this country and abroad—but I hate to see them kept so closely confined. It is not good for the animals or for the spectators. It is uncomfortable for the animals. Did you ever see that poor anteater pacing up and down in his tiny cage? Couldn't he have more space? Now my point is this: we have a responsibility toward animals that we capture and keep for our own amusement and education. If the nation's capital houses Zoo animals this way, millions of visitors will think this is all right and proper because Uncle Sam permits it.

MR. BUSH: I agree, sir.

SENATOR PETERSON: Thank you, Mr. Bush. What you

have said is very interesting to me. We will have to see if we can't work out something that will help you, help the animals—and still not cost too much.

As Senator Peterson sat at his early nineteenth-century desk in the Senate Chamber that afternoon following his morning of committee hearings, much of what he had heard was stirring around—fermenting—in his ever active brain. He knew that, somehow, the problems facing both of the committees this morning could be solved. He felt that idle, mischief-making boys and unhappy zoo animals could help each other. He must figure out a way—for his daughter's sake and for the sake of all the future young men and women of America. It was a challenge that he must face. It was a grave responsibility for the Congress. The power of a United States Senator must be used for good in all of his waking hours. Through him, the people's wishes must be made known. And the people ardently wanted an end to this sickness of so many of its young people.

With that, the earnest young Senator turned and paid attention to a fellow Senator making a speech on the floor of one of the most important forums of modern times.

9

Adventure in the Moonlight

Jebby awakened with a start. His heart was pounding. Something unusual must have roused him. Had it been a car back-
firing down on Connecticut Avenue, four flights below? Or was
it a noisy mockingbird, her chest bursting with melodies in the
spring night? Or could it have been the wild mare calling him?

Whatever it was, he didn't hear it again, but, with the moon's
silvery light flooding his bedroom, he couldn't get back to sleep.
He lay there restless. He wondered how many other people were
awake in the large apartment house? His mother was in a deep
sleep. He could hear her breath rise and fall. As he thought of all
the people in the apartment sleeping, snoring, turning, twisting,
he longed to be out in the fresh night air. This was the time of
the year he used to hear the Whippoorwill at night. Over and
over again, the little gray bird that nobody ever sees would repeat
"Whip Poor Will, Whip Poor Will." This call made some people
so sad that they wanted to close their windows—but not Jebby. He
was sad without it!

Now he remembered how he used to walk in the woods and
fields near North Mountain in the spring. He liked to hear the tree
frogs, spring peepers they called them. And the bullfrog down at
the cow pond croaked so loud that Grandmother had called him
"old man of the mountains." There was an old barn owl, too, that
used to keep a sharp eye out for the night creatures—quicker than

a chicken hawk she was, too.

The night sounds in Washington were still unknown to Jeb-by. But if there were a variety of night sounds at the farm, there should be even more in the Zoo at night. Jebby began to wonder what the caged animals did at night. Did they sleep or did they pace up and down, roaring or howling at the moon? The idea of going to see for himself began to take form. If he slipped out quietly, Mother would never know.

Thought was swiftly translated into action. Jebby slipped out of bed and reached for his khaki shorts and a T shirt. Then he put on his dark blue sneakers without bothering with socks.

He tiptoed out of the apartment, for he did not want to wake up his mother. He hurried down the corridor, took the stairs to the lobby, slipped out the door, then crossed the deserted avenue. The Zoo's large iron gates were locked, to keep out auto traffic. They were always locked at sunset. But it would be easy to get into the Zoo on foot, Jebby knew.

He climbed a hill next to the Zoo that ran level with the chain link fence. Here, it was easy to slip over. Anybody could do it; but it was not likely that many people were that anxious to visit the Zoo at night.

Jebby landed behind the yak paddocks. Major MacFae had told him that these strong beasts from Tibet were happiest when they lived and worked at more than ten thousand feet. The shaggy yak paid no attention to the boy as he walked stealthily behind their paddocks.

He had no fear of rousing either the yak or the buffalo, but he hoped that the zebra wouldn't start running up and down as he passed. That Mexican burro, Pedro, he was one to be watched, though. At the joyful sight of a man or a boy, he would start the most noisy hee-hawing, and he might arouse the guards.

Once he reached Isabella's paddock, in a very out-of-the-way place around the bend, he would be safe, Jebby knew. So far, so good, Jebby thought, as he walked softly through the moonlight. And then, suddenly, he felt his skin prickling with fear and his heart started thumping faster. A furious scream split the night ... then another! It was followed by an eerie yowling, more lonesome-sounding than a dog baying at the moon.

Which animal had screamed that way? Was it a hyena, monkey, or one of the cats like a lynx or puma? It reminded him of the screeching of the bobcats at night behind Grandmother's house. There it went again! Jebby could feel the goose flesh rising on the back of his neck. Now, once more, that yowling, howling, long and low. Were these mating calls or caged animals' rage by moonlight caused by the sight of a rabbit or some other free night creature hopping by? When he heard the howling again, Jebby decided, though he certainly couldn't be sure, that this was the call of the gray timber wolf. And the wolf was furious because he couldn't reach out and grab a tantalizing cottontail.

The yowling and screaming stopped. And the wolf of the wild

returned to being a passive, pacing caged wolf again. He must have realized, Jebby thought, that howling in the night would never unlock his cruel cage.

And the screeching puma had given up, as he had given up many many times before, and silenced his mating call since there was no mate to answer him.

Night meant different things to different animals. For the timid, night was a protection, like Zorro's black cloak. But for the stronger ones, night was the best time to hunt and kill. The fox and the owl did their best work at night, Jebby remembered.

As he turned the curve leading to Isabella, the boy had a strong feeling she was expecting him.

The mare lifted her head as he approached. He whistled softly the traditional call that sounded like "Here ... here ... here."

Jebby could scarcely believe his ears, but Isabella was nickering! He was sure of it! Was she answering him?

The boy approached the wire fence around the wild mare's paddock. He put his hand through the mesh and spoke softly. "Here, old girl, here. I have something for you."

It was only a piece of carrot, a rather old one, that he had found in his pants pocket. He tossed it to her—and she ate it!

This was progress, Jebby thought. It must have been that special Mongolian grass the other day that had convinced her. Now, maybe, she would eat anything he offered—at least, he hoped so.

This was another step toward his goal of taking her to green pastures someday, somehow. He tried to stifle the thought of riding her, although it was hard to believe she was a killer mare.

The night air smelled so good that Jebby just couldn't turn back to the apartment house right away. He headed toward Rock Creek, instead. This was the time of the herring run. Thousands of herring were on their way from their spawning ground up in Maryland. Soon the banks would be filled by day with men and boys, fishermen with snag hooks. The birds were quiet, but Jebby wondered if soon some of them—especially the gold finches—would be somewhere overhead, returning from their wintering grounds in the South. Some would probably stop here for days, he figured, because they always did over in Virginia, before going further north.

The moonlight made the dogwood trees, some opening their waxen blossoms, look as if they were floating through the air. The tall trunks of the sycamore trees were so pale and ghostlike that they almost gave Jebby the shivers. But the scent of wild wisteria reminded him of his home on the farm and he wasn't afraid. As he entered the Black Horse Trail, he paused. A mother possum was crossing his trail, five babies following her.

Seeing her living the way an animal is supposed to live—even with its dangers of being picked off by an owl—made Jebby feel sorrier than ever for the little caged animals in the Zoo's Small Mammal House. That place didn't even have windows! The anteater and pampas cats never got to feel the earth beneath their feet, to smell the night air, or even to put up a fight against a natural enemy.

Jebby didn't like to admit it to himself, but he knew he was headed toward the yurt. He must be careful not to awaken Dorje Lama by stepping on a stick.

As he approached their dell, he noticed that little pieces of cloth about the size of small handkerchiefs were tied to branches of the trees. Some were red, others blue or yellow. He didn't know it then but they were typical Buddhist prayer flags. The Lama had attached them to the branches as Lamas had done in Central Asia for hundreds of years. But before Jebby could really wonder what they meant, he had reached the dell. And what he saw there took his breath away!

Dorje Lama, wrapped in flowing red robes and wearing a peaked golden hat, sat cross-legged on a red rug in front of his yurt. He was mumbling strange words—"Om Mani Padme Hum ... Om Mani Padme Hum ... Om Mani Padme Hum...." All the while, he twirled a little gold and silver object in one hand. It looked rather like a baby's rattle. And with the other he fingered his string of prayer beads.

Dorje Lama did not appear to see Jebby. His face was expressionless. But the boy knew that the Lama could see him, unless he was too absorbed in his ritual, because he had one foot out in the dell.

Jebby stood there, motionless feeling very out of place in this exotic atmosphere just wearing khaki shorts and a T shirt. He could smell incense burning inside the yurt (although he did not know until later what the heavy, spicy odor could be). And their aluminum-framed yurt looked very handsome in the moonlight—especially Grandmother's hooked rug with all the red roses on it that hung in the doorway.

Jebby continued to stand quietly. After all, Dorje Lama was a Buddhist Lama. The boy did not know to what a Lama prayed or why he prayed, but that was not the important thing. The important thing was that the Lama needed a secret place to make his spirit strong.

Dorje Lama, Jebby realized, was at prayer....

In a few minutes, the Lama finished chanting and lay aside his prayer wheel. This was the object that looked to Jebby like a baby's rattle. "Welcome," he said, "welcome to the temple of Lord Buddha." He pressed his palms together in the usual Buddhist greeting, and Jebby did the same.

There was no surprise in the Lama's voice. He accepted Jebby's post-midnight appearance as a normal occurrence. He rose from golden cushions that Major MacFae had brought to the secret dell. "Enter, please," he invited as he folded back the rug door.

Jebby entered, blinked his eyes, unbelievingly and blurted out, "Wow!"

Could this be their simple, hand-built yurt? The walls were hung with glistening scrolls of silk and parchment on all of which were painted pictures of the same man—always sitting cross-legged. This man, Jebby was to learn later, was Lord Buddha himself.

On one side of the yurt there was a small altar on which a statue of the seated Buddha was placed. It was carved out of a shining

*Dorje Lama, wrapped in flowing red robes, sat cross-
legged on a red rug in front of his yurt.*

pink stone, known as rose quartz. On each side of the Buddha burned incense candles and their smoke gave off a spicy, heady scent. It made Jebby slightly giddy.

The smoke from the candles and the little charcoal stove drifted out of the hole in the top of the yurt.

"Sit down, please," the Lama said. "Have cup of tea?" He poured Jebby tea into one of the green jade cups.

"Thank you," said Jebby as he sat down on the beautiful dark red rug. It was the one Major MacFae had called the Royal Bokhara.

"You come as first guest to Lord Buddha's Temple," Dorje Lama said.

"I didn't mean to interrupt you and bother you at your prayers," Jebby said. "I came to the Zoo because something woke me up and I was restless. Then I decided to come on here and see the yurt."

"Young boy wanted to be near wild horse?" the Lama asked.

"Yes, sir," Jebby replied.

"Wild horse need young boy. Boy need wild horse."

"Why," Jebby exclaimed, "I thought you said that these horses had been treated so cruelly by man."

"Yes, horse throw off and fight any man who try to ride her. But horse need man, too."

This was mysterious double talk that Jebby could not understand.

"Every living thing need another living thing. Wild horse have nobody. You kind to wild horse."

"Oh," Jebby said. He was beginning to understand in a blind, groping sort of way. Isabella might remember her mother and her brother, who once were here at the Zoo. Her mother died and her brother was taken away. And now she was lonely.... Jebby, unable to fathom his own thoughts, gave up trying.

"You like animals, Dorje Lama?" he asked in a half questioning way.

The Lama nodded his head in assent. "Buddhists do not kill animals. Buddhists should eat no meat."

Jebby looked surprised, but then realized that he knew very little about the customs of other people. Living in Shenandoah County all of his life had taught him a lot about animals and plants. He understood about the changes of the seasons, and how the chain of life is built, each link depending on the other. But about the life and beliefs of people from distant lands he was very ignorant. He should not be that way. Well, there was one way to find out—and that was the direct way.

"Tell me about Buddha," Jebby asked Dorje Lama.

10
Dorje Lama Tells About Buddha

Dorje Lama's story began with the birth of a prince in the high-mountain kingdom of Nepal. The mountains within this distant Asian land are covered with everlasting snows and few men have scaled their slippery heights. The highest of these mountains was to be named Mount Everest in years to come. But most of them would always keep their ancient names, like the massive Kanchenjunga, meaning "Spirit of the Mountains." Nepal lies next to the land of the Hindu, called India, and to the mysterious kingdom of Tibet. And not far away was the home of the emperors of ancient China.

The young Nepalese prince was born six hundred years before another boy, called the Prince of Peace, was born on the far side of these mountains.

The teachings of these two young men—which are the same in many respects—have helped men and women throughout the years to find strength to carry the burdens placed on their backs by misfortune and despair. The Western world followed the way of Jesus Christ. In Asia, many persons, like Dorje Lama, followed the path laid down for them by the young prince of Nepal, whose name was Siddhartha Gautama.

Gautama had from birth everything anybody could desire. His boyhood was filled with fun and games. When he reached manhood, he married a beautiful girl, and they had a fine young son.

His parents stayed well and lived near them.

The prince had a different palace for the cold winter months, the hot months and the humid rainy season. He had precious jewels to run through his fingers and he had lotus filled pools, dear to the Eastern heart, in the courtyards of his many palaces.

Around him was only happiness. No tears. No illness. No worrying. But the young prince was puzzled. Something disturbed him. He could not believe that life was this way everywhere. He must find out about life outside his princely territory.

So Gautama rode out into the world.

It was then that he saw human suffering for the first time. He saw a man too sick to walk. He saw an old man, bent and feeble with age. And he saw a dead man.

When the young prince returned to the Palace, the memory of these unfortunate people haunted him. He could not rid himself of the worry as to why some people should have a happy life and others a miserable one. There must be some reason. He tormented himself with this question. He must find the answer. And the answer would never come, he realized, if he continued to live a life of luxury.

Gautama made up his mind to solve the riddle of life, even though this meant leaving his home forever. He did so sadly, but he knew he must follow his destiny.

He wandered for six years over mountains, through jungles and across the hot-baked plains.

First he followed the practice of some of the Hindu holy men of India by denying food and water for his body. These men thought that by doing this their minds would become sharper. But this left Gautama weak and wretched. Without food to sustain him, his mind became dull. He knew this was not the way to find the truth.

Then he tried the other extreme—a life of eating rich and heavy foods and drinking the fermented grapes that made a wine so clear and sparkling and tasty that some men thought in it were the answers to life. But the wines did not bring an answer—only headaches.

Gautama then tried the middle way.

He ate enough so that hunger would not press against his sides. His mind now was not too weak to think. There seemed to be a balance, at last, between mind and body.

As he wandered over strange lands, he came to place called Bihar. There, he found a special tree. It was called the Bodhi Tree.

He sat there for forty-nine days and nights. He reflected on the suffering he had seen—the crippled, the lepers with their noses eaten away and their fingers mere stubs, and on the starving children whose rice bowls lay empty by their emaciated bodies.

Why? ... Why? ... Why? ...

He had many visions as he sat under the Bodhi Tree. An evil devil tempted him in a dream, offering him all the wealth of the world if he would give up his search for the truth.

Gautama said, "No."

Then the devil attacked him with storms of hail and jagged, terrifying lightning. But Gautama remained steadfast under the Bodhi Tree.

The wind whipped his body that was bare to the waist. The hailstones beat against him and lightning daggers played around his head.

But in all of this evil darkness of night and storm, the prince began to feel that the truth lay soon ahead.

And when the storm cleared, leaving the atmosphere washed bright and clean, Gautama knew that today he would find the answer.

When Dorje Lama came to the climax of his story, Jebby could not wait, he blurted out, "What was it? What did he discover?"

"Be patient, small son, patience," the Lama replied.

Jebby held his tongue.

"The prince made a discovery that the suffering in life is caused by selfishness and wrong craving," the Lama continued. "When man does things only to help himself, the day comes when he must suffer for it. This craving, this selfishness, is a sin.

"When Gautama got up from under Bodhi Tree, he was not

called Gautama any more, but Buddha. That means 'enlightened one.'"

"Oh, this prince became the Buddha!" Jebby exclaimed, gazing at the rose quartz Buddha statue on the small altar.

"Yes," said the Lama as he arose from his cross-legged position and walked to one of the paintings on cloth that he had hung on the wall of the yurt. It was a picture of a wheel with eight spokes.

"This wheel is very important to the Buddhists. Remember about the hub and spokes and follow their rules and you will have good life."

Jebby wondered what the wheel had to do with the young prince who had sat under the tree during the terrible storm.

"Now look at the wheel," Dorje Lama told him. "Buddha said that the hub of the wheel stands for truth, because truth never moves.

"Each spoke is the same length, so think of justice when you see the spokes. Justice is equal for rich man or poor man. If rich man do wrong, his punishment is the same as for poor man who does wrong.

"But spokes also mean something very special. Each spoke is a rule of Noble Eight-fold Path. If man follows these rules, he will not crave anything and then he will not cause suffering for himself and his family."

Dorje Lama indicated one spoke after another, and, as he did so, he told Jebby the rules for which they stand:

"Right knowledge
Right intention
Right speech
Right conduct
Right means of livelihood
Right effort
Right thoughts
Right concentration"

"These rules," Dorje Lama said, "will keep young boys out of trouble."

"I don't crave anything, Dorje Lama," Jebby said, "except maybe I wish sometimes that I lived in the country again. And then sometimes I think I would like to ride that wild horse."

"Boy, stay off wild horse," Dorje Lama warned. "If you crave to ride wild horse, big trouble for you."

Dorje Lama's voice was stern. There was something about his tone that frightened Jebby. This was a serious moment, he realized. He was getting fair warning that he must use self-control and banish this thought for all time.

"You treat nature right, she will treat you right," the Lama admonished. "Wild horse, like nature, can not be treated badly. Treat her badly, break her spirit, she break your body."

"Yes, sir," Jebby said in a weak voice. "I'll try not to think of riding the wild mare."

The night suddenly became more mysterious as the Lama picked up his prayer wheel, twirled it around and around and mumbled over and over, "Om Mani Padme Hum ... Om Mani Padme Hum...."

Jebby knew the time had come to go back to his world. He could not stay here in this world to which he did not belong. He was only a privileged visitor.

He rose from the silken cushions, clasped the palms of his hands together and bowed himself out of the yurt into the night made dark by the clouds covering the quarter moon. He headed back up the Black Horse Trail, strong in his promise never to ride Isabella.

11

Research and a Dream

Loss of sleep the previous night made Jebby's eyes heavy. And the voices of his teachers lulled him as he sat in the various classrooms. All he could do was keep his head up and pretend to pay attention—but his thoughts were far away from algebra and history. He was lucky that none of the teachers happened to call on him during what seemed an endless day.

When school was out, he went straight to the apartment to make a telephone report to his mother at the office. He looked longingly at his bed and wished he could fling himself down for a quick nap, but no, it was more important for him to go to the yurt for his second Shao-lin lesson. He had noticed Shad eyeing him calculatingly today—an evil eye, too! The Caps were just waiting for an opportunity to catch him alone, he was positive. So he had to be careful every time he went to Rock Creek Park—to be sure they didn't see him. They would show him no mercy. Until he could learn these Shao-lin holds, he would not be able to defend himself against several at a time. And even then–

Major MacFae and Dorje Lama were sitting cross-legged on the handsome dark red rug, enjoying a cup of tea when Jebby arrived at the yurt.

"You look sleepy, lad," the Major said. "Have a cup of tea. That will freshen you." He reached for the pot.

After Jebby had taken the steaming cup, the Major picked up

a large book from the rug. "I visited the British Embassy library and found a book for you on the cave paintings," he told the boy. "Thought it might come in handy when you write your essay. It has lots of photographs taken inside the caves."

"Oh, thank you, sir!" Jebby exclaimed as he reached for the large volume. It was bigger than a geography book. He quickly riffled through the pages. And then his eye fell on one picture that made him call out excitedly, "Look, Major MacFae, look, Dorje Lama—that's our horse, that's the wild mare! Look, see the mane, the head, the dark legs—everything is just the same!"

The two men bent their heads over the picture of a horse that did, indeed, look very much like Isabella.

"Did cave men really paint these pictures?" Jebby asked.

"Well, that's what everybody thinks," the Major replied.

Jebby rubbed his forehead reflectively. "Where are those caves anyway?" But without waiting for an answer, he said, "We have lots of caves out near where my grandmother lived—Luray, Endless Caverns, Shenandoah Caverns—Do you suppose I could find pictures inside any of them?"

"I rather doubt it," the Major replied. "I don't think anything has turned up here in America like in France and Spain."

"France and Spain," Jebby repeated, "they're a long way from China and Mongolia, aren't they?"

"Yes, rather," said Major MacFae. "Thousands of miles."

Jebby was bursting with questions. "Why did the cave men paint these pictures of horses and other animals on the walls?"

The Major paused a moment before answering. "You won't like this, feeling the way you do about the mare, but cave men hunted these horses. We think they ate them, for we have found piles of bones. They speared them sometimes. But often they would drive the terrified animals over cliffs, then finish them off after they fell."

The thought of such barbarity made Jebby more indignant than squeamish. "Gosh, they were awful—but I still don't see why cave men drew these pictures of horses, even if they did hunt them."

"Cave men hunted these horses with spears."

Major MacFae took out his pipe, stuffed it with tobacco and tapped it before carefully lighting it. "Well, Andrews," he replied, "if man of today knew the answer to that question we would be that much wiser. But we do have our theories."

"What are they?" Jebby asked.

"This fellow, Cro-Magnon man they call him, probably did not live in these caves, although most people think he did. He used them as a combination of an art gallery and a place to practice a kind of magic."

"What kind of magic, Major MacFae?"

"You know I told you these fellows were hunters. Well, they evidently decided it would bring them good luck if they painted pictures of these creatures on the cave walls, with darts, like arrows or harpoons, sticking in their bodies."

The Major turned to a page in the large book of pictures of cave paintings. "Look here, lad."

Jebby saw the arrows and spears sticking in the hindquarters of bison and horses in the picture. "Look, at this one," he said. It showed a reindeer with an arrow pointing to its heart. The poor creature's knees were buckling under him.

"There were all kinds of animals then, weren't there?" Jebby asked. "But what about the dinosaurs?"

"Dinosaurs disappeared thousands and thousands of years before these animals and men came along. These men of the Paleolithic Age seem ancient to us, but dinosaurs are even more ancient. But to answer your question about other animals, probably the saber-tooth tiger and the mammoth—that's the elephant with the shaggy long hair—could have lived then."

Jebby was turning the pages slowly. He saw picture after picture of cave horses just like Isabella. But none had men on their backs. Jebby was satisfied that she really was too wild for cave man to ride. He was trying to puzzle out this mystery when the Scotsman clapped him on the back.

"Up with you now," commanded the Major, turning from scholar to soldier. "Time for your Shao-lin lesson."

At the same moment Dorje Lama arose.

"Today, young boy try to knock Lama off feet. Push this way...."

Jebby got up and took a deep breath. He was still sleepy from last night, but he knew he must take his defense lesson seriously. The Caps could strike again at any time.

When the lesson was finished, Jebby took up the book and propped himself up against a pine tree to look at it again. But as he turned the pages, his back started to slip down gradually and the pictures and print began to blur before his drowsy eyes. He yawned and decided to stretch out for just a few minutes...

Isabella, Isabella, how fast you are trotting, and the horse behind you, and behind you.... Look at them coming, all alike, a whole battalion.... Far out front galloped the leader. His head was held high ... he was reddish tan ... and his black tail stretched out behind him. Galloping along the flanks of the long lines were young stallions ... hundreds of horses ... hundreds ... thundering across the sandy wastes....

Their hoofs beat a steady rhythm ... there were no other sounds ... only horses, sand, and a cloudless sky. On ... on ... on— And then, a loud neighing rent the atmosphere. Like a relay, it was picked up by each young stallion until the whole world seemed to be filled with the cries of wild horses.... The mares were calling shrilly to their foals, "Danger, danger, danger, stay close!"

The long column shifted from the steady trot to a full gallop. They left the sandy wastes and headed to fields grown high with bluebells and yellow flowers.... The sky began to change ... clouds appeared. They churned in the heavens and the horizon began to darken. Against the darkness of the sky, the horses became like pale galloping ghosts....

The lead stallion veered to the left. The line, as if one body instead of hundreds, hugged close, very close to him.... He turned again ... and again ... he was trying to confuse the enemy in pursuit.

The enemy followed on the backs of horses ... horses no longer free but broken to the will of man. Their riders held the reins with one hand and long poles like lances in the other. On the ends of the poles there were nooses....

The stallion darted one way, then another, and the frightened, faithful herd followed.... One mare stayed close to his side as he ran and circled and tried to throw the hunters off the track.

Again the stallion gave a signal ... a mighty neighing that swept like a whiplash across the backs of his following herd. Their pace quickened as they reached mountains rising up before them. The stallion headed into a pass between rocky cliffs, calling the others to follow him.

The mounted men tried to go along after the others. They whipped their horses unmercifully ... but the long line had slipped through the pass and now were entering a land of golden sunset....

The men on horseback could not follow. The approaches to the pass were guarded by little dragons. The hunters pulled up tight on their reins when they saw the dragons hissing at the entrance of the pass. Finally, they wheeled around and headed back....

The galloping wild horses slowed down to a steady trot after they emerged from the pass.... The stallion had brought his herd into another time and world. They had crossed the dragon-guarded barrier leading into the past. This was the Stone Age world!

As they trotted forward they passed strange animals not seen in their other world of desert wastes and grasslands. Here were heavy creatures with long curving tusks and shaggy coats, camels with shaggy silvery hair, stags with wide-spreading antlers that seemed to reach the sky. The horses passed the black and golden tiger. His long saber-teeth were like ivory sentinels guarding a massive citadel....

Ahead of them, crouching in the tall grass was another curious creature. His body was draped with a bear's skin, and around his neck hung a necklace of animal teeth. He carried a spear tipped with bone....

His eyes were fixed on the sleek, beautiful mare trotting close behind the stallion. Her head was high and proud, her muzzle was as white as the snow on the mountains far behind, and her flanks were sleek and the muscles rippled strong and round as she moved forward. The streak down her back was black as the mark of coal. Her eyes were brown and soulful as a fawn's ... she was a happy mare, home—at last—with her beloved. She was Isabella....

The crouching, two-legged creature was close now ... close enough to release the spear poised and ready for its flight to the mare's heart. His arm was bent back and his eyes were fixed on the spot....

"Isabella, Isabella!" The call came from a boy wrapped in a reindeer skin, with long black hair streaming down his back. As he called, he leaped forward.... He landed on the back of the man with a spear, knocking it from his hand. Then he bent back the threatening arm, holding it there while the line of horses trotted past, never noticing the man and boy of the caves as they wrestled in the tall grass.... Isabella passed with them, never knowing.... Now, far behind her the boy and man rolled in the grass, the harsh blades cutting into their backs. The boy's breath came in gasps as they rolled ... rolled....

"Ho there, lad, having a nightmare?" Major MacFae called. The Scotsman had suddenly noticed that the sleeping boy's legs were jerking and that he was breathing heavily and moaning slightly.

Jebby opened his eyes and shook his head. The Major's voice served to pull the curtain on that exciting scene of his dreams which had taken him across the time barrier. But he still found it hard to believe that he wasn't rolling down the hill with the cave man who wanted to kill Isabella.

"No time for nightmares in the bright daylight," the Major joshed.

Gradually, everything came into focus for Jebby. He was still at their secret place, their Xanadu, in Rock Creek Park. He was still a fourteen-year-old boy and high-school student who loved horses and life in the woods. He was not a cave boy, after all, even if Isabella, in a way, was a cave horse.

"Oh, it must have been a dream!" Jebby said.

He shook his head once more and looked around him, as if he were searching for the twentieth century.

"But, boy oh boy!" he sighed. "It was some dream."

12

Jebby's Essay

"Cave man painted her pictures on the walls of caves."

That's the way Jebby's essay began. He was standing before the class, reading it aloud, for it had been chosen one of the best by Miss Pepper.

Jebby had pieced together the tales told him by Major MacFae and Dorje Lama and what he could find in books in order to write his essay.

His opening words seemed to catch the attention of the class. Even Shad looked up from reading a comic book he had stuck in front of the English literature textbook.

"But you can see her today at the National Zoo," Jebby continued. "The Zoo animal I have picked for the subject of my essay has drawn the interest of scientific people and people who like history. But no one has ever written a poem or a play about her. She is the true wild horse." Jebby pronounced the words proudly.

"You might find a few of her kind still running wild in a country between China and Russia called Outer Mongolia. This horse is one of the ancestors of our modern horses. Her ancestors first came from America, but they weren't really horses. They weren't much bigger than collie dogs and were called eohippus. They moved from Alaska to Russia on a land bridge, over the waters called the Bering Strait. They lived in Asia for thousands of years and gradually changed into horses, like the one here at the National Zoo.

"There must have been several kinds of horses in ancient times, but there is still a lot of mystery about this. We do know that they interbred and produced the different sorts of horses we have today. This Mongolian horse is the only living exact type of those early ancestors left in the world today.

"You may wonder how I know she is such an ancient horse. The answer is that we have pictures of her that were drawn long, long ago—at least, many of them look like the Mongolian wild horses. The cave men painted her picture on the walls of their caves. There are a lot of these caves with pictures of animals in France and Spain. The cave that has the most pictures of these ancient horses is at a place called Lascaux, in France.

"The story of how these Lascaux cave pictures were found in 1940 after about twenty thousand years of nobody knowing they were there is very interesting. Some French boys, about the same age as the boys and girls in this class, were out hunting one day with their dog whose name was Robot. Well, Robot disappeared down this hole, and the kids couldn't find him. They whistled and whistled and finally figured he must have fallen in. So the boys went down in there. They found their dog all right; but it was those paintings on the wall that surprised them. They had matches with them, so they wouldn't get lost. They lit some and spotted these pictures of all kinds of animals, painted in red, yellow, brown and black. Sometimes the animals had spears sticking in them. Our wild Mongolian horse in the National Zoo looks exactly like some of these paintings on the walls of that cave in Lascaux. Experts came from everywhere, after these French boys told their schoolteacher about their find. These experts said the pictures were painted by Stone Age hunters.

"Funny thing, these horses can't be found in Europe today, except in zoos, but maybe if a person hunted terribly hard, he might find them out in the real no-man's land of the world. I have been wondering about them a good deal, and I believe that a lot of them ran out of grass out there in Mongolia, so they came over to

Europe, looking for something to eat.

"Some of them stayed in Outer Mongolia, though, because there was just enough food to support them. This is so far away that very few people ever go there. It was really by mistake that the true wild horse was found in 1898, which is not very long ago when you think of how many years back these horses go. A Russian named Colonel Nicholai Mikhailovitch Przewalski (I looked it up to get the right spelling) was hunting for wild camels, but, instead, he found the body of a wild horse.

A few years later, a man who collected wild animals for zoos heard about these rare horses and he wanted some, so, he sent a hunter out there in Mongolia, to round up a few. It was a very cruel roundup, because these animals don't give in to man easily. Nobody breaks them and rides them, once they are grown. They may kill any man who tries it. Lots of people think that tigers and lions are the most dangerous animals, but these wild horses can be just as dangerous. Nobody dares ride them.

"This is one of the most important animals in our Zoo. And

she is certainly my favorite." Jebby read the last sentence of his essay with particular warmth and sincerity and sat down.

"That was fine, Jebby," Miss Pepper said. "I learned things I didn't know before." She noticed that Shad was waving his hand in the air. "All right, Shad, what is it?" she asked.

"The kid is crazy," he declared, "that horse is wild like a tame Shetland pony."

"She is not," Jebby replied hotly. "She has thousands of years of wildness behind her. And you could ride her just as quickly as you could ride the tigers out there at the Zoo. You are writing about the tiger, aren't you? Well, why don't you ride her?"

The class laughed. This was a choice argument, and, so far, Jebby was coming out ahead.

"You think you're so smart, so intelligent," Shad retorted, pronouncing the word in-TELL-igent. You don't think nobody can ride that horse. Don't kid yourself, I'll ride her myself and have a picture to prove it. Picture won't be painted by no cave man, neither."

Miss Pepper rapped for attention. "Another word, Shad, and you will go down to the principal. And watch your grammar, too. Katie, come up front, please, and read us your essay about the albatross."

Jebby tried to listen to Katie, but he was so annoyed with Shad— and with himself, too, he couldn't concentrate. He shouldn't have put in his essay about these horses not being ridden. He had left himself open to a different kind of attack. Not only would the Caps keep on trying to get him sometime, now, they would be out to get the horse also. If two or three of them worked together, they might be able to hold her with ropes for a quick minute for Shad to climb on her back.

What he meant in his essay was that nobody had been able to ride a wild Mongolian horse the way they rode regular horses.

The question now was: when would the Caps strike?

13

The Caps Strike

The Dall sheep had an easygoing disposition, so seeing Jebby and Major MacFae in her paddock in the middle of the night disturbed her very little. The two friends crouched behind the flowering spice bush in the corner of her paddock, which was next to that of Isabella.

Jebby wasn't sure how the Caps planned to seize the mare. It would be no easy matter. But they must never even get started. He would land on top of the nearest one before any of them had a chance to try to mount Isabella. Even to get a boy on the mare's back for a moment, to take a quick flash picture, would mean a terrific struggle—of this Jebby was sure. Whatever the outcome, she would distrust man more than ever before. All the confidence that she had placed in him since he and Major MacFae had fed her the Mongolian grass would be destroyed. And the boys might be hurt, too. If they were killed by the "killer horse" ... well, Jebby didn't like the Caps very much, but he certainly didn't want to see them killed!

Katie had tipped him off that the "gang" planned to strike to-night. She had heard it from one of the girls whose brother was a member. Katie said they would arrive about midnight.

Katie had made Jebby promise that, when he got home after stopping the Caps, he would telephone her, no matter how late. All he had to do was dial the number, let it ring once, then hang up. She would stay awake, waiting. If he didn't call, she would know something had happened.

She had promised not to tell her father about the affair unless it was necessary. Of course, then it might have been too late to be of any help. Jebby had wanted to handle the Caps himself. Although he trusted and respected the police, he felt that this was strictly a struggle between himself and the gang. He could never have put it into words, but Jebby felt that, once that he and the Caps could reach a "stand-off"—that is, nobody being top man—then maybe life between them at school and in the neighborhood might be better. In the future, they could go their way and he could go his way. Tonight was the final testing. To have the police interfere would not settle matters for good—only postpone the settlement. Having Major MacFae there was not like having outside interference. He was involved in this as much as Jebby and the Caps. Perhaps Major MacFae was having second thoughts as to whether he should go along with this struggle between the boys. This was a question Jebby was not going to ask. But he suspected that the Major was searching his soul as to whether this contest between Jebby Andrews and the Caps might get out of hand. But, after all, the Major was a man of the wilds, deserts, hills and had lived a life as free as a nomad's, so perhaps he wanted to see a boy have one adventure on his own before he did everything by the rule book. At least, that's the way Jebby judged it. And he tried to convince Katie that was the way it had to be. But still, down deep inside, they knew that they were on dangerous ground for boys and girls.

As the Major and Jebby crouched there in the darkness—the moon was not yet up—their ears became attuned to every night sound in the Zoo. The sharp bark of the little foxes in their pens down the hill broke the stillness every once in a while. And the old screech owl would give one of her eerie cries.

Jebby's muscles began to ache. Staying in the position of a coiled spring was not easy. Major MacFae got up and stretched his legs. Jebby realized that the former cavalryman's war injury bothered him if he stayed in a cramped position for long.

"Doubt if they're coming tonight," the Major whispered. "War of nerves, you know. Think I'll look around a bit."

Jebby didn't follow the Major as he left the sheep's pen to go on a reconnaissance survey. His dream was still very vivid. He wondered if the cave boy of his dream, who landed on the cruel hunter's back, had waited long in the tall grass, too?

He thought of many other things. Suppose the boys did get a picture of Bo or Shad on the horse? It would make him look pretty silly at school. Suppose Isabella was docile and she allowed one of them to mount her with ease. But Major MacFae and Dorje Lama were not the only ones who had said no one could ride her. He had talked to her keeper and he said that she was the meanest thing in the Zoo and that he wouldn't stay in the stall with her, not for a second. She had tried to bite him and kick him several times!

Suddenly, the soft atmosphere began to change. It became charged with a feeling of electricity. The animals down the line must have been put on guard. Jebby could almost feel the impulses, signaling danger. A bird roosting in the large tree above the paddock flew over his head. He could feel the soft flutter of wings.

Then, suddenly, a door slammed. In the darkness of Isabella's paddock there was a boy!

The coiled spring within Jebby was released and he sprang over the barrier. Swinging his right arm around the boy's neck, he pulled him to the ground.

It was Shad, and he fought back like a tiger. Jebby thought he had him, but Shad broke loose and landed a blow on Jebby's right eye. But then Jebby grabbed his opponent's wrist and bent it back the way Dorje Lama had taught him. It got Shad off balance and then Jebby threw himself on him. And in a moment they were rolling in the dusty paddock. They bumped against the side of the mare's stall door that had just been slammed tight shut.

As the two boys struggled, Jebby could hear the mare inside the stall, snorting with alarm. Then he caught hoarse half whispers, half shouts rasping through the darkness.

"We've got her!" a boy called. "We've got her!"

What did it mean? Jebby relaxed his grip on Shad. He must save the horse. But as he loosened his grasp, Shad pulled his arm free and aimed his fist at Jebby's jaw. But Jebby sidestepped neatly and grabbed his opponent by the shirt. Shad's punch landed in the air. He was off balance and Jebby had his big opportunity. He tossed Shad head over heels into the side of the paddock. It was a combination of superhuman strength and the trick Dorje Lama taught him.

Shad landed on the ground with a thud. He lay in a heap, the breath knocked out of him.

Jebby rushed to the area behind the mare's paddock. What he saw there filled him with fresh concern. Isabella was in the "squeeze box." This, he knew, was a strait jacket for animals! The stall on wheels had been pushed up to Isabella's stall door, and she had been driven into it. Bo and Lucky were turning the screws on the movable sides of the box, so they would press against the mare and hold her in a vise.

Why, oh, why, Jebby wondered in that fleeting instant, hadn't he thought of this line of attack? He had seen the old squeeze box sitting in the field behind the hoofed animals' paddock. Zoo keepers had used it in the days before the invention of the tranquillizer gun for immobilizing animals when they wanted to inoculate them or treat them for illness or injury. If the squeeze box were used unwisely, a Zoo keeper had told Jebby, an animal inside it could be squeezed almost to death. And it always caused panic as the wooden sides pressed against the trapped creature's body.

Isabella was breathing hard. She could not move. Bo was trying to get a bridle over her head, which protruded over the front of the box. She was tossing it up and down, with her ears flattened back.

"Stop, stop!" was all that Jebby could call out. He was nearly breathless from his struggle with Shad. And now he faced both Bo and Lucky. Where was Major MacFae?

"Stop!" he shouted again and charged Bo, knocking the bridle out of his hands. Bo rushed him in turn. Jebby grabbed his arm, stepped sideways and, with a slight turn of his own body, flipped Bo over to the ground. The Lama's special trick again! But Lucky was after him now, and Jebby was even more breathless than before! He needed help.

Suddenly, Major MacFae stepped between the two boys. On returning from his little stroll to ease the cramp in his game leg caused by waiting so long, he had heard the commotion and came as fast as possible. The Scotsman grabbed the boy and tossed him several feet onto the turf.

In a matter of seconds, however, the Caps were back at them. Jebby felt a blow hard in his face, another to his stomach, but he remembered all the rules that Dorje Lama had taught him. *Keep relaxed. Let the enemy use his own strength against himself.*

Meanwhile, Shad had recovered from his hard fall and rushed out of the paddock. But Jebby, light on his feet, ducked as Shad tried to deliver a blow and grabbed him by the shirt a second time. Shad fell forward.

Major MacFae and Jebby were winning the battle when, suddenly, all of them heard a sound that made them pause. There was the crash of hoof on timber. The five, spellbound, could hear wood splintering, planks being torn from their nails, then a series of sharp blows—Isabella was kicking herself free!

At that moment, the clouds covering the moon drifted away. All of them—Major MacFae, Jebby, Shad, Bo, Lucky—were transfixed by the sight of the struggling mare. She had kicked out most of one side of the box, on which the Caps had not yet tightened the screws but, to escape, she would have to clear an iron bar. She braced herself. Her muscles swelled and rippled under her mouse-colored coat, now wet with sweat. The mare did not hesitate. She was ready to call on the strength of her wild ancestors of the Central Asian steppe. She sprang into the air with a defiant snort, and cleared the barrier. It was a phenomenal jump—a leap to freedom.

She was free!

No man, no boy, no friend, no foe had done this for her. She

She sprang into the air with a defiant snort, and cleared the barrier. It was a phenomenal jump—a leap to freedom.

had freed herself from the cruel cage—and now her hoofs were on the springy turf.... She paused for an instant, then tossed her head, snorted again and was off at a gallop into the night.

Jebby streaked after her, the fight with the Caps almost forgotten. His eye was swelling, but he could scarcely feel the ache.

14
Search for Isabella

Jebby's heart pounded and his breath grew short as he ran down the wooded path in the pale half-moonlight, searching for Isabella.

She was nowhere to be seen.

He had unhappy visions of the wild mare galloping down through the park onto the slick city streets. Police cars, with their wailing sirens, might chase her and she would slip and break a leg. The policemen would look her over, shake their heads hopelessly and then, with one bullet, put her out of her misery. They wouldn't know she was the true wild horse—a jewel among animals. She would seem to them just a horse with a broken leg, escaped from a riding stable, who must be saved from further suffering. Jebby's thoughts galloped even faster than the wild mare herself.

Where could she have gone so quickly, he wondered as he stumbled on. He stopped every few minutes to whistle "here ... here ... here," never believing for a second that she would answer with a soft nicker. But he had to do something. He was the cause of this and he must not allow any harm to come to her.

As he slowed down to a walk, he suddenly had a feeling he was not alone. Something or somebody was following him. The clouds had covered the moon again and everything seemed black and spooky. He was afraid to look back. It was a steady tread—and it was coming closer and closer!

Just as he got up his courage to turn his head, someone spoke. "Aye, laddie," rang out a familiar voice, "you need a ride."

A warm wave of relief surged through Jebby. Looming up in the darkness was a huge, ungainly shape. It was Haggis, with Major MacFae aloft. She came closer and the boy could feel her warm, smelly breath. He was too worried about the mare to express his surprise over the camel.

"Oh, Major MacFae, she's gone!" he cried. "Will we ever get her back? Can we go and get her?"

"That's what I plan to do—with your help," the Scotsman answered reassuringly. "First you must climb aboard."

"I can't get way up there."

"Not necessary, Haggis and I are coming down to you." With that, he said words that sounded like "sook, sook, sook," and the camel, like an ancient house in an earthquake crumbling to the ground, came to her knees.

"All right there now, Jebby boy, you're a skimpy lad, so fit yourself in here with me between Haggis' two humps," he said.

The boy could never remember the old Scotsman calling him Jebby before. It was usually "laddie" or "Andrews." And his voice seemed so gentle, like a grandfather's, when he said, "Jebby boy." Major MacFae evidently understood how badly he felt and was trying to make it easier.

Jebby couldn't speak except to say, "Yes, sir," as he climbed behind Major MacFae, with Haggis' second hump close against his spine.

"Now hold on tight," the Scotsman instructed. Jebby put his arms around Major MacFae's waist. Nevertheless he was unprepared for what happened next! At first he seemed to be rocked back so far that he was afraid he would go over the camel's rump, as if it were a sliding board. He held on tightly to Major MacFae. Then, as quickly as he had been jolted backward, he was now propelled forward. His full weight must be enough to knock Major MacFae over Haggis' neck.

But none of these dire things happened. Instead, Jebby found himself—his stomach somewhat churned—sitting aloft on the camel, the ship of the Gobi desert, who tonight would serve as huntress for a wild mare of the Mongolias in Washington, D. C.

"We will find the mare," Major MacFae stated in a confident voice.

"Oh, do you think so?" Jebby asked with a note of longing and anxiety in his voice.

"We will head Haggis down to the creek. Maybe Isabella is getting a cool drink."

The camel made her way slowly down the steep path to the Rock Creek valley, which was damp and cool and filled with pleasant scents of moss and old leaves. The trio passed the paddock that held the little white-tailed Virginia deer. Sensitive to any noise intruding on their secluded pen, the gentle creatures trotted up to the wire fence. Their delicate ears were alert and their soft brown eyes full of wonder.

Jebby wished they could tell him if the mare had passed that way.

"She's gone further than I thought," the Major said, half to himself, half to Jebby. "But never mind, we will find her."

Jebby swallowed hard. His mouth was dry and his throat so tight it ached, but he said nothing. Haggis lumbered on at a rough, uneven pace, along the narrow path. Soon they came to a fork in the trail. One led to the street. Jebby could hear the roar of a foreign sports car zooming down the four-lane parkway that linked Connecticut Avenue with Sixteenth Street. The other path would take them to the upland forest. Which path had Isabella followed, he wondered. The one leading to the street was the most traveled, because it was used as an exit from the Zoo.

"I doubt if we can find a hoofprint," said Major MacFae, "but let's try the high road. I don't want to get us exposed out there on that parkway. Wish for the best, that's all we can do now."

This was a dreadful moment! The mare had disappeared completely, but the searchers pushed doggedly on the upland path, neither trusting himself to speak.

"Don't worry, son, we will find her," Major MacFae said. "She likes company—at a distance. She will realize that she is lonely in a few minutes and she will stop running and look around her. She will stop and listen. She will be glad to see us. Watch!"

"Gosh, I hope so," Jebby replied.

Major MacFae could feel the tenseness of the boy's body next to his. He was sorry for him and blamed himself. The thing to do now was to reassure Jebby and get his mind off the mare—even for a moment.

"You know, laddie, camel riding might have become an everyday thing in the United States if camels had taken on in this country." The Major paused and didn't finish his story. Something had attracted his attention.

Then, suddenly, Jebby could feel Major MacFae heave a sigh of relief.

"Good show, good show," he said. "We're on her trail now."

"But how do you know?" Jebby asked.

"Fine thing these clouds have moved," the Major answered, "or we might have missed it."

Missed what, Jebby wondered—then he knew. On the path ahead was a steaming pile of manure. Never before had Jebby's eyes beheld such a welcome sight. "That means she's not far ahead," he exclaimed.

"My guess would be the picnic grounds," ventured the Major. "I don't think she'll try the seesaw and swings of the wee lads and lassies." He chuckled. "But a fair supply of grass may be growing there."

"I hope so, oh, I hope so!" cried Jebby, wishing old Haggis would speed up.

Finally, their path reached a clearing, and there, in the pale moonlight, they could make out the shadowy form of the wild mare.

"Steady now," the Scotsman advised. "Don't call out and startle her. She has been through a pretty bad experience and she must still be nervous. She doesn't quite know what to do with freedom."

As they approached, the mare raised her head. She tossed it up and down nervously. And then Jebby whistled softly, "here ... here ... here." Her ears pricked up ... she remembered.... She knew her

friends were here.

The Major headed Haggis back toward the Zoo.

"I think the mare will follow us. Just whistle and she will come. She doesn't want to be left alone."

"Oh, Major, Major, sir," Jebby pleaded, "let her graze a little while longer, even if it's just beaten up grass where the kids have been playing ball. It is the first time—maybe ever—that she has eaten any growing grass. When we get her back to the paddock, she will have to stay there. The night guards won't miss her," Jebby pushed his argument. "If they check her paddock, it will be from the front. Nobody will go around back and see the squeeze box and the stall door open and all. Besides, she stays in her stall a lot at night and that's where they'll think she is when they go by."

Jebby's arguments were made convincing by the pleading tone of his voice. Major MacFae didn't need much convincing, anyway. He remembered from his distant youth a phrase that went something like this: "The heart has reasons that reason knows not of." And this boy was speaking from his heart. The Major, too, hated to see an animal shut up, leading an unnatural life in a Zoo enclosure. So somehow they would get her back and straighten up all evidence of the escape, the Major felt. Maybe these feelings that everything would turn out well came from days of being out in the vast empty lands where he could get in tune with life-flowing currents. Somehow the current seemed to be flowing in favor of Isabella.

But a fourteen-year-old boy and a retired British major little thought they could change the National Zoo's method of exhibiting its animals. Even the directors and keepers were unable to do that. This was a matter for the Congress of the United States—for all the people—to make it a better Zoo where animals could live a more natural life. Tonight, all this sympathetic pair could think of was helping one animal and not what they could do for all.

The Major took off his fuzzy tarn o'shanter and patted the top of his white head. He was worried and undecided and, somehow these futile gestures helped.

Jebby waited expectantly.

"All right, all right," the Scotsman finally agreed. "But, not here. This place is too open. Look," he indicated the road that flanked the picnic area, "somebody will see us here—and then our troubles will really start!"

"But where shall we go?" Jebby asked.

"On the far side of the yurt," Major MacFae replied, "there's a field—grass is tender there, even a few buttercups this time of year."

"Oh, good, let's go there!" Jebby was grinning broadly.

"The kindhearted cavalryman-explorer-naturalist turned the camel's head toward Black Horse Trail—and Isabella followed!

15

Isabella Says "No"

Dorje Lama heard the noise of the camel and the horse breaking through the underbrush, so he came out of his yurt and waited for them in the dell. He may have been surprised by this nocturnal visit, but his face remained inscrutable. He greeted his two friends with the Buddhist hands-folded gesture.

"Mendi, mendi," he said.

"Now for a spot of tea," Major MacFae said to Jebby, "but first we must give Haggis her peas and take the horse to the pasture."

Jebby wondered where they would find peas, but, before he could raise the question, the resourceful Scotsman was calling to Dorje Lama. "I say, old man," he addressed the Kalmuck lama as if he were a fellow countryman, "would it be too much bother for you to poke around on the left side of the yurt and see if I left a bag of peas there?"

"Sain, Sain," Dorje Lama replied, meaning "O.K." He complied quickly with the request and emerged from the yurt with a shopping bag like the one the Caps had knocked open that first eventful day. It obviously contained peas. The Major reached down for it and gripped it securely.

"Now we're off to the pasture. I'll be back in a moment for tea," he told Dorje Lama.

"Camels don't graze at night, so that's why I have the peas on hand down here. But we will let the mare eat this good grass while we have a spot of tea."

He gave a signal to Haggis. The venerable camel folded to her knees and the two slipped from between her humps. "Now, I'll tether her here," the Major said as he tied the long reins to a sapling. He poured the peas that were in the shopping bag on the ground in front of her. "Don't worry about the mare. She will stay rather close. So come along now, Andrews."

Jebby hung back, watching Isabella, who was on the edge of the field. "If it's all right with you, sir, I don't believe I care for any tea tonight," he said to the Major. "I'll just stay out here and look around for a little while."

The tea-thirsty Major shrugged his shoulders slightly. "As you like," he agreed. "I sometimes forget that you're not an inveterate tea drinker like Dorje Lama and myself." He chuckled and added, "Sorry, I don't have a bottle of pop."

After the Major left to return the few yards to the yurt, the mare stepped forward into the field that was glistening with buttercups in the pale moonlight. Such luscious grass was a new experience after years in a barren paddock. She stepped forward gingerly ... then put her head down. But she did not eat. Instead, the mare's knees gradually began to fold under her. Jebby watched with delight as, deep in clover and buttercups, she began rolling happily on one side, then the other. There's nothing better for a horse—and a boy, too—than a good wallow in the grass. Jebby knew this from experience in the country. He perched on an old stump on the edge of the meadow and began to chew on a tender piece of grass.

As the boy sat there, looking at Isabella, who was now back on her feet and busily grazing, he had a chance to think about the last ten days. They had been exciting days, all right. During that time, he had been able to realize the very first wish he had made when he came to Washington. Seeing the wild mare enjoying that good grass was his dream come true. He had certainly craved that— perhaps craving might not be the right word. You crave when the chief benefit is for yourself, not for someone else, he figured.

In spite of his delight, Jebby felt sad, too, because, now that he had brought Isabella to a green pasture, would this be the last time? How would he ever be able to do it again? Getting old Haggis out undetected and riding down through the park with the mare following was mighty complicated. It was a miracle no one saw them. He toyed with the idea that it would be for the mare's own good if he could ride her down to this pasture on other nights. He wouldn't need a saddle, and he could make a bridle out of rope. All he would need would be a bit. He could buy one cheaply out of his pocket money, he felt sure. Of course, the old camel was ridden with just a halter, but Jebby was doubtful whether Isabella would respond only to that—provided she would respond to anything.

As Jebby woolgathered about riding the wild mare, the desire to do so grew stronger. It had been months now since he had put a leg over a horse or pony, and for a boy who has ridden all his life, riding is almost a necessity.

But, Jebby reminded himself, he had forsworn his ambition to ride Isabella, for she was wild. He had told the entire class so. He had told the Friends of the Zoo so. He had told everyone about the cave men not being able to ride her ancestors. He knew, deep down, that Major MacFae and Dorje Lama spoke the truth about this.

The still of the night was broken only by the comforting sounds of the mare chewing and moving her feet forward every few minutes while she grazed. Jebby thought of his strange, mixed-up dream about himself as the cave boy. Didn't the cave boy have a desire to ride one of these wild horses, too? Maybe he had saved the mare from the hunter because he wanted to ride her. Jebby wondered what would have happened next in his dream if he hadn't waked up when he did. Would the long-haired cave boy have caught the wild mare and become her master?

Her secret master ...

Master ... master ... master.... The repeated words rang down hidden corridors of Jebby's mind, and he did not try to dismiss it. He liked it. He was master of nothing any more—not a dog, nor a cat, nor a mouse.... Nor was he master of himself, for, suddenly, Jebby jumped up from the stump, ran across the field and, with one leap, landed on the mare's back!

His legs gripped her tawny sides. His heart began to soar in triumph—forgotten were his good resolves, the Buddhist teachings against craving, the early admonitions of his grandmother, Major MacFae's Scotch burr ringing out, "Ah, lad, she's a killer."

But that sense of triumph lasted only a moment—no longer. Isabella jackknifed her body in a perpendicular buck, and the boy soared through space ... through the moonlit night.

The wild mare had rid herself of twentieth century man, just as her ancestors had rid themselves of cave men more than twenty thousand years ago. This boy on her back was a violation of centuries of independence. She was a true wild horse, and no foe—not even a friend—could change her.

Jebby lay among the buttercups and clover that had once

The wild mare had rid herself of twentieth century man,
just as her ancestors had rid themselves of cave men . . .

looked so soft, but now were only a hard bed for a bruised body, while the mare galloped across the field, flinging her heels in the air. Then she was circling back. The friendly nicker with which she had once greeted the boy was replaced by a shrill, knife-sharp whinny.

Jebby half heard her. He tried to rise, but was still too dazed to get to his feet.

Isabella galloped about the field, then headed toward the boy, like an arrow speeding toward its mark. She had no special hatred in her heart for this gentle boy who only wanted a horse to ride. She could not help herself, for she was the true wild horse, defending herself against man, the would-be conqueror.

So Isabella headed straight toward the half-conscious boy. It was too late to deflect her course by any normal means. Her hoofs thundered against the turf, her breath came in gasps.... She was a force of nature and of time that must move forward ... forward ... forward....

Then, suddenly, high-pitched screams rent the air. Like demons from hell let loose on the land ... like the screams of the Furies of ancient Greece ... like banshees and goblins, all rolled up in one!

The shrill notes hit their mark, for the mare tossed her head in fright, which made her change her course slightly. She wavered and hesitated.

This gave Major MacFae an extra moment to step further forward into the golden meadow, beside the fallen boy's limp body. And all the time he was blowing his bagpipes with every bit of breath within him. These challenging pipes from the Highlands screamed as loudly as ever they did when those gallant Scottish warriors, the "ladies from hell," in kilts and sporrans, marched forth to do battle with the devils of a thousand fronts.

The mare swerved and galloped past the boy, who had so nearly been pounded to death by her savage hoofs.

At that moment, Dorje Lama, his red gown streaming behind him, swooped Jebby up in his arms. The boy's head fell back limp-

ly.

Together the two men carried Jebby back to the yurt and laid him gently on the red Bokhara rug.

Major MacFae went outside and dipped his handkerchief into the fresh, cool spring. Returning, he laid it on the boy's forehead. Jebby moaned as he tried to open his eyes.

"No hurry, lad," Major MacFae said gently. "You will be in fine fettle soon."

At the reassuring sound of the Major's familiar voice, Jebby tried again to bring himself back to reality. He moved his head and moaned again. Finally, he opened his eyes and looked at the anxious-eyed Major, then at the impassive face of Dorje Lama. He half smiled at them.

"I reckon," he announced weakly, "that Isabella said, 'No!'"

16
Katie Gives the Alarm

Staying awake for Jebby's telephone call was a great struggle for Katie that night. She had propped up two big pillows behind her head and tried to concentrate on the book before her ... but the print would start to blur ... and she could feel herself slipping down on the pillows. Twice she got up and dashed cold water on her face and ran some over her wrists. If her mother had not been out of town, visiting Aunt Marie, who was sick, she wouldn't have gotten away with leaving her light on for hours past her bedtime. Her father was in the next room, asleep, blissfully unaware of his daughter's vigil. She was waiting for Jebby to dial her telephone number and so signal her that he was safe and that the Caps had been chased away from the wild horse's pen. But the call didn't come—that ringing bell which would bring her Jebby's message that his mission was safely accomplished.

At two a.m., Katie's sleepiness suddenly left her. Worry had made her wide-awake and was forcing the decision that she must do something to save her friend. She knew he had not forgotten to phone, because he had solemnly promised he would, and he was not the kind of boy to forget his promises. She must go look for him. He might be lying unconscious or hurt.

Katie got up quietly, dressed quickly in a skirt and sweater and canvas shoes and tiptoed to the front door of the house. But, as she put her hand on the knob, she drew back. The darkness outside seemed so big and black. No, she couldn't do it. She couldn't go it alone. This admission to herself of her fear made her cheeks burn bright with shame, but she knew she couldn't master that fear quickly or completely, so that there was only one thing to do. She would tell her father.

She turned and hurried to his room. Bending over his bed, she patted him gently on the shoulder.

Daddy, Daddy," she said, quietly but urgently. "Wake up, Daddy, please. Something's happened to Jebby. I know it. I just know it."

"What's this? What's this all about?" the Senator demanded, rousing himself.

"It's Jebby," Katie repeated. "We've got to go help him."

Senator Peterson shook his head and sat up. In a few moments, he was poised on the side of the bed, listening intently to his daughter's story. She explained quickly how the Caps had threatened to ride the wild mare and get a picture and prove that Jebby was wrong in his essay.

Being a man of quick reflexes, the Senator decided he must swing into action immediately. "Bring me a flashlight out of the kitchen, Katie," her father instructed "while I get dressed." He slipped into a gray sweat shirt, old slacks and brown loafers, splashed some water on his face and was ready to go. But all the while he was doing this, he wondered whether he should call the police and the boy's mother before going off—just he and Katie, on their own.

He discarded both ideas because he was a man who had always made his own investigations, gathered his own facts before getting everyone else involved and excited. Sometimes it took more time to explain what the problem was than to solve it. And in this case, he was not real sure any problem existed. For all he knew, Jebby was safely asleep in his bed, so why call his mother—he, a stranger, at this hour of the night—and frighten her out of her wits? He would find out soon enough. It was just a short drive to the Zoo.

The two rushed outside, jumped into the family car that was parked in front of their house. The streets were empty, so it only took a few minutes to drive to the Zoo.

Although Connecticut Avenue was lined with parked cars belonging to the residents of the apartment houses across from the Zoo, he was lucky in finding a parking space. He pulled up the handbrake, and the two jumped out and rushed to the iron gates. They were locked.

"How will we get in?" The Senator asked his daughter.

"I'm not sure," Katie answered hesitantly.

"Well, we'll look around a bit and find a way," her father said with determination.

He paused and quickly sized up the lay of the land. The moonlight was a great help. Don't worry, we'll get in," he reassured her.

"Let's go up that hill and see if we can't get over the fence there? It may be level with the bank at that spot. Probably it will be a pretty good drop on the other side, but I believe we can make it."

This was exactly the same route Jebby and Major MacFae had taken for getting into the Zoo—and also the time he visited Isabella. The Caps had used it, too.

The Senator and his daughter climbed up the hill and swung over the fence—but they were not as lucky as Jebby and the others had been, for, as they dropped down into the Zoo property, long fingers of light caught them. The Zoo patrol car was moving its searchlight up and down the paddocks, following the usual protective routine.

"What do you think you're doing?" a blue-uniformed police officer demanded as he jumped out of the Zoo prowl car.

"We're looking for a missing boy," Senator Peterson replied.

"A missing boy?" the officer repeated. "Quit your kidding."

"Yes, officer, a school friend of my daughter's."

"Lost in the Zoo after midnight?" the officer demanded, "A likely story!"

The Senator began to explain, but the officer took him by the arm. "That's your story, but I think you had better come along and see the lieutenant and do your explaining to him. But first, what about some identification?"

"I am Elias Peterson, 815 Lancaster Terrace."

"Occupation?"

"Member of the United States Senate."

The officer repeated the question.

"United States Senator, I told you," Senator Peterson said firmly.

"Cut out the kidding! Let me see your identification."

Senator Peterson reached into his hip pocket for his wallet—but there was nothing there! His pocket was quite empty.

"I am sorry. I left it home when I slipped into these old slacks so hurriedly to come look for the kid."

"What's the kid's name?" the policeman asked.

"Jebby Andrews."

The officer grunted in disbelief and, with a wave of his arm, directed the Senator and Katie to the waiting prowl car.

Meanwhile, Jebby was lying out flat on the red rug in the yurt, where his two friends had placed him and slipped a rolled-up sheepskin under his head. The Lama had put a steaming hot poultice on his forehead, explaining, "Tzetz-serba, made of dandelions."

Jebby lay there quietly, wishing that it was all a dream. It wasn't his throbbing head, aching shoulder or sore leg that bothered him so much. He would rather have all his bones broken than to have broken his promise. Broken bones would heal faster than a broken vow. The worst part of it was that he had no one to blame but himself.

"Would the lad like a good cup of tea now?" asked the Major.

Jebby smiled feebly through lips swollen from the fight with Shad. "Thank you, sir."

He almost wished that the Major and Dorje Lama would say, "I told you so!" But both of them were so gentle and considerate.

"I didn't know you had bagpipes," Jebby mumbled to the Major as the Scotsman handed him a cup of tea.

By a stroke of good luck, I brought them down here yesterday," the Major explained. "Thought we might have a concert some day—and maybe the lad would like to learn to play them, eh?"

Then the Scotsman, in a rare gesture of tenderness, patted the boy's arm. "Don't worry, laddie boy, we'll have that concert and the special feast—a true Mongolian stew—even yet."

Jebby sighed. He had messed up everything in the worst way! Everything had been going along so well down here at the yurt. The Caps had been a problem, but tonight he had even put them in their places, thanks to the Lama's training in self-defense. He really had a great chance to get the wild mare back to her paddock when they found her at the playground. But selfishness had ruined that. He hadn't intended to be selfish. From the very first, he had been mixed up in his feelings toward the wild mare. First, he had only wanted to take her to green pastures. But all the time, inside him, there had been that nagging insistence that he ride her. He thought he had conquered it. He had told everyone she couldn't be ridden. By learning about Buddha and self-control, he had tried to tell himself he craved nothing. But there had been that one moment when he couldn't resist—that one awful impulse that had overcome him—a sense of craving. It was a moment of selfishness that he felt he would never live down, even if he went on to be one hundred years old.

The shame seemed almost too much to bear. The Caps would have the laugh on him. And Katie would think he was a double-crosser—Katie!

Jebby lifted his head from the sheepskin, sat up waveringly on the Bokhara rug and clasped his aching head in a moment of despair. "I can't call Katie!" he cried.

"Who?" asked Major MacFae.

"Katie Peterson. I was supposed to call her when I got home and to let her know everything was O.K. What time is it anyway, please?"

The Major pulled out his gold pocket watch. "It's now three o'clock, lacking five minutes."

"Oh, my gosh!" Jebby groaned. "Too late now."

"Now don't be off borrowing trouble. The lass is probably

asleep," Major MacFae said reassuringly.

Jebby only accepted his friend's explanation in a half-hearted way. But even Major MacFae couldn't reassure him about breaking his vow not to try to ride Isabella.

"I shouldn't have done it, Major MacFae," he blurted out finally. "Why couldn't I have left well enough alone?"

The Scotsman rose, lit his pipe and walked to the doorway of the yurt, his head bowed in thought. He took a few puffs on his pipe. Then he removed it from his mouth, held the bowl in his fingers and pointed the stem at the unhappy boy.

"I'll tell you something, Jebby, lad. You were only acting out things nature's way."

Jebby was puzzled, but he was all ears.

"You are a higher form of nature than the horse. You are man, you know. You can think abstract thoughts. You can see around curves. Animals cannot always do this. Now you were trying to break nature to your will. In this case, your wild mare, your Isabella, was nature, too—a somewhat lower form—and she wanted her will to be the stronger.

"You see, young man, this was the old contest being played out once again—the old contest of man seeing whether he can triumph over primitive nature.

"And you couldn't do it, could you? But there's no reason to be ashamed. Even the biggest dam builders don't always succeed when nature's floodwaters are high. You have learned a lesson, Jebby. Mastering nature is not the important thing, but learning to live with it, understanding it, that is important. You and nature will both win that way. I think you have learned a good—a valuable—lesson."

Jebby listened quietly. The words did ring true. Man shouldn't try to bend everything to his will. If man ruled with an iron hand over all the earth—the animals, the birds in the sky, even the worms in the ground—well, what kind of world would that be? Jebby knew he didn't want that kind of world. But, on the other hand, man couldn't let nature walk all over him either. There had to be some kind of balance, he reckoned. This was Grandmother's kind of thinking—"Live and let live," she used to say.

One thing Jebby knew for certain. He did not hate Isabella—or blame her. He respected her. She had lived up to her deserved reputation as the true wild horse. She had shown the Caps and she had shown him that she was the real thing.

Jebby and Major MacFae realized they couldn't stay in the yurt any longer. They must return Haggis and Isabella to the Zoo well before daybreak. In fact, even now, their absence might have been discovered by the night patrol.

"How does the laddie feel? Any bones broken?" the Major said in a joking manner.

"Well, sir, my arms still move." Jebby grinned bravely. "My feet move, too, so I guess I'm all in one piece. But my head hurts and I ache all over."

"Bruised all right. Quite a fall when the mare tossed you off her back. Do you believe you could sit on old Haggis without tumbling? We must get those two animals back to the paddocks."

"Do you think Isabella will still follow Haggis?" Jebby asked. "And how will we get her in her pen? The squeeze box—or what's left of it—is in front of her door."

"Take one thing at a time, laddie boy," the Major advised. "We'll find a way." It was clear that the Major was not too sure of the details of how they would achieve their goal, but immediate action was necessary.

The Major and Dorje Lama gave Jebby a hand and pulled him to his feet. For a moment, the Royal Bokhara rug with its handsome designs swam before the boy's eyes. He took a deep breath. He wasn't going to give in. He clenched his teeth and squared his shoulders. "I am O.K.," he said resolutely.

Dorje Lama and Major MacFae relaxed. They had stood there, each tense and almost holding his breath, but each in his own way had faith that Jebby would not give in to the bruises of his fall and have to be taken off to the hospital.

Haggis was on her knees just outside the dell, and the Major sat on her back, then urged, "Climb aboard, son, and we will go up to the pasture and get Isabella."

Jebby slipped between the humps, every muscle aching. Although he kept a tight grip around the Major's waist, the jolting of the old camel as she rose to her feet didn't startle him so much this time.

Haggis was headed up to the field. Jebby held his breath because he wasn't sure Isabella was still there. But he should not have worried. The mare was in a horse's seventh heaven of grass and buttercups. And she was still munching away steadily.

As he whistled "here ... here ... here" Jebby felt a wrench of regret that he was taking her away from all this. At first she didn't respond to his summons. Then she raised her head and replied with a soft nicker. How different she sounded compared to the raging proud beast of an hour before who would have trampled the very life out of him!

"She will follow," Major MacFae said confidently. He turned Haggis' head back in the direction of Black Horse Trail, and repeated the words, "tak, tak, tak" to get her moving.

The wild mare followed.

The camel lumbered along in her usual leisurely manner. The group hugged the rim of a precipice as they went down hill and up. Now they were approaching one of the open areas that crossed the parkway. So far, Major MacFae had always been lucky in not having any cars pass when he reached this exposed spot with Haggis. But in this predaylight hour, his luck didn't hold, for as the little cavalcade emerged out of the wooded area, the beam of a searchlight caught them. They were pinned down! There was no escape.

The motor of the car was quiet. Men in uniform came running across the field.

"Stop, stop!" one of them shouted.

The first one to reach Haggis grabbed the camel's reins. While he did that, another police officer tried to throw a rope over Isabella's head, but she swerved and bolted, speeding back toward the woods.

"What do you think you're doing?" demanded the Sergeant who held Haggis. In the next breath, he ordered Jebby and Major MacFae to dismount.

"Get down," he repeated, when they did not obey. "You heard me the first time." He jerked the reins as if he were trying to pull the old camel to her knees.

Then, Major MacFae spoke. "When you take your hand off the reins, we will get down," he said quietly.

"I am giving the orders around here," the officer replied. "I am charging you with the theft of Federal property—that camel and that horse."

Major MacFae looked down at the sergeant and asked, "Now, Officer, you'd not want to annoy the camel, would you?"

The policeman disregarded the remark, giving another tug on

*Major MacFae looked down and asked, "Now, Officer,
you'd not want to annoy the camel, would you?"*

Haggis' reins.

"Camels can get angrier than people," the Scotsman warned. "And when they do, anybody within spitting range had better watch out!"

"Spitting? What are you talking about?" the officer replied in disgust.

"And when they spit on your clothes, it takes weeks to get the smell out ..." the Major elaborated.

Jebby, all the while, said nothing. Mostly, he was worrying about Isabella, who had dashed off in panic, but he did remember Major MacFae once telling him about ill-tempered camels who spat up a foul-smelling green stuff from their stomachs.

The officer was growing more and more annoyed at this deliberate defiance. Jebby could see how tense he was. It would probably only be a minute now before Haggis would spit. But what would trigger her off? Or was it all a gamble, a bluff on the Major's part?

But at that very crucial moment one of the other policemen broke in with the warning, "Sergeant, you had better watch out. The man up there ain't kidding. These camels can spit up something awful."

The sergeant looked at him and frowned, but he realized his fellow officer must be speaking from firsthand knowledge. He took his hand off the camel's reins, muttering, "I am not afraid of you or that camel either, so no false moves to get away!"

"Thank you," said Major MacFae.

He prodded Haggis with his left toe and pulled slightly on her reins, giving the signal for her to come to her knees. During all this time of struggle, the camel, through her heavy double eyelashes, had been gazing disdainfully at the sergeant. Now, her neck more proudly arched than ever, she came to her knees with such grace that even a caliph of Bagdad or emperor of China would have been proud of such a mount.

At the very moment when Major MacFae and Jebby were dismounting, they heard the screeching brakes of a car coming to a sudden stop.

A spotlight played over them again and Jebby heard a girl's voice calling from across the field, "Jebby, Jebby! Are you all right?"

It was Katie!

17

Surrounded!

Katie dashed across the field well ahead of the men who piled out of the Police Scout Car. She could see Jebby and Major MacFae atop the camel, which was coming to her knees.

"Jebby, Jebby," she called as she arrived at the scene. Much to Jebby's surprise, and even her own, she flung her arms around the old camel's neck. It was such a relief to find Jebby that her eyes filled with tears, best hidden in the camel's hair.

Then she turned and looked at the boy.

"You've been hurt! Your eye is closed and your shirt is torn. Oh, Jebby, what did the Caps try to do?"

Jebby slipped painfully off the camel but tried not to show that it hurt to walk.

"Oh, I am all right," he said. "I am sorry I didn't get to telephone you."

He couldn't really be mad with her for setting the alarm as they had agreed that he would notify her when he drove the Caps away from Isabella's paddock.

There wasn't much time for them to talk because the men in the car with Katie had now arrived at the spot where Haggis knelt.

The sergeant was talking loudly.

"Yes, sir, I am charging them with theft of Federal property. Horse thief and camel thief, both of them," he blustered. "The horse ran away."

A tall young man with a sweater over his pajama top spoke curtly to the sergeant.

"I'll take charge now, Sergeant."

"Yes, sir. Yes, Mr. Bush," the sergeant said to the Zoo director. "But I just want to say this...."

"Thank you, Sergeant. Senator Peterson and I can get the details and decide whether to prefer charges."

In the meantime, Major MacFae stood quietly by the camel's head.

"I am Fergus MacFae," he said and proffered his hand. "This scrape—theft, or whatever you want to call it—is my doing."

"Major MacFae of the famous Central Asian Expeditions?" the Zoo director said as he thrust forth his right hand. "This is a great pleasure, sir. I heard you were in the City getting a medal, and I have been looking forward to meeting you. I've read your books and wanted to talk to you for years about the Ovis polii, Marco Polo sheep. How I wish we had a few in our Zoo. And the Himalayan panda, we don't have a one."

Mr. Bush was clearly carried away by meeting the famous explorer-scientist. But he checked himself.

"Excuse me, sir, I would like you and Senator Peterson of Wyoming to meet. And this is his daughter, Katie."

The Major and the Senator shook hands with a warm vigorous clasp as Jebby and Katie looked proudly on. Jebby was amazed to hear that the Scotsman was a famous author, too. He had felt from the beginning that Major MacFae was keeping something back.

"The lieutenant at the guard station called me at home a little while ago and told me that one of our men had brought in the Senator and his daughter," Mr. Bush explained further. "The lieutenant didn't know whether to believe the story or not. But I came right over—didn't take time to dress properly." His pajama collar showed that his night wear was red, white and blue striped.

"Senator Peterson and his daughter told me the whole story. I know the Senator all right. Have appeared before his committee. We phoned the boy's mother to verify whether he was missing. I hated to call her. But fortunately she remained calm. I've sent one of my men to get her. And by now she's got the message by police car radio that he's safe." The Zoo director was clearly nonplussed by the whole incident, for he added "When the Senator told me this story I would never have dreamed that I would have found you in the middle of it...."

"Aye, a real adventure, we've had," the Major said. "I think the laddie here will be all right but needs a spot of rest and another poultice for his eye."

The Zoo director looked at Jebby closely. "Looks like you've been roughed up a bit."

"Yes sir," Jebby replied in a low voice. He was debating whether he should say that part of his poor condition was due to being tossed on the ground by the mare as well as the struggle with the Caps. It was always best to make a clean breast of things. So he swallowed and spoke.

"I had a little fight and I had a little fall, too, Mr. Bush." Then he added, "but I am all right. The mare only did what comes naturally."

You mean you rode the wild horse?" the Zoo director exclaimed in amazement. "Holy smoke!" He clasped his head. "And you weren't killed?"

"I was on her back just for a second," Jebby replied. "I didn't mean to, but I've been thinking about her so much and about cave men and all that. I just couldn't help it. She seems so friendly ever since Major MacFae fed her that special steppe grass. She got so she knew me."

"You don't mean it," the Zoo director replied. "She is one of the most valuable animals in our collection, but a she-devil. I am surprised she followed you down here. Frankly I wouldn't go in the paddock with her. She might trample me."

Jebby said nothing about how the mare tried to stomp him. Major MacFae remained quiet, too. This, they knew, was their secret. Other people wouldn't understand and even the Zoo director might punish her in some way, treat her like a criminal.

"She's a rough one. I guess my men will have a hard time getting her back to the Zoo," Mr. Bush said. "So the best thing to do is to shoot her with the T gun."

With that pronouncement, he called one of the guards standing close by with a coil of rope in his hands. "Jenkins, do you have a T gun in your patrol car?"

"No Sir," he replied, "but I can get one quick from the guard house."

"Well, get it and send the other men out in the park to search for the mare. She must have really high-tailed it away." He paused and asked Jebby, "Where do you think she is?"

Jebby's face had gone pale and he stood there clenching his fists. T gun ... shooting the wild mare ... No, no, it couldn't be true. Those words echoed in his mind.

He didn't answer Mr. Bush.

Major MacFae broke the silence. "Did you say T gun?"

"Tranquillizer gun, sir," replied the Zoo director. "We use it frequently for stubborn animals we cannot handle and that we want to move from paddock to paddock. Shoot one of the little darts in the hip and the animal quiets down in a jiffy. Makes them mild as mice. Why after we use the T gun on the mare, this kid can ride her with ease."

"Oh, but I don't want to ride her," Jebby said.

"But I thought you did try to ride her," the director replied. He was baffled.

"Yes sir, I did. But she was her real self then, her natural self. That T gun will dope her and make her something she isn't. I don't think it would be fair for me to ride her then."

Major MacFae had lit his pipe and stood there quietly, puffing by Haggis' head, watching the little drama unfold. The boy had learned a great lesson and he was already applying it. He had learned a true respect for the wild. He would not take unfair advantage of the mare while her wildness was subdued by drugs. That kind of achievement would be cheap. Jebby was playing the game of life fair and decent. Life might be hard for him sometimes because some people played the game by selfish rules. But Jebby, the grizzled Scotsman knew, was going to play it by nature's rules.

"I think this is the best way, the most humane way," Mr. Bush explained. "Otherwise we would have to lasso her and then maybe hog-tie her. And you know what that is. She might even break a leg while the wrangling is going on and you know we don't want that to happen...."

Mr. Bush could hardly finish his sentence because of the screech of brakes of the police patrol car that was drawing up behind the others down on the road. A uniformed policeman and a woman came running toward them. It was Jebby's mother. She was a slim dark-haired woman of about forty years of age. Everyone standing there could see how much she and Jebby resembled each other—dark hair and eyes and even features.

"Are you all right, son," she called as she reached the group. Her voice was calmer than anyone expected it to be.

"Fine, Mother, just fine," Jebby replied bravely.

"The message came on the police car radio that you were all right, so I reckon I shouldn't have asked you," she said as she hugged her son. She didn't kiss him because she knew that boys of that age hated displays of affection in public from their mothers.

"I always knew you loved horses, Jebby—but not this much. Your father was the same way and Grandmother, too. But you shouldn't have come out at night this way, darl...." She caught herself because calling her son "darling" in front of everyone would make him blush. "You're not back up at Stoney Creek and North Mountain, Jebby," she admonished him. "We let you wander around up there to your heart's content. But it's different here. You'll have to learn that, son."

At that moment a shout went up from the nearby woods. It came from the guard named Cornelius Page.

"Look, quick, there's another one," Page was shouting. "Got him, got him good, too—he's a tough one all right," he continued. Since Page was supposed to be searching for Isabella no one knew who or what he was shouting about.

"A two-legged varmint if there ever was one, found him hiding in the bushes watching all you folks!"

Jebby knew even before Page emerged from the woods who the varmint must be. One of the Caps. But which one?

The answer wasn't long in coming. Page was dragging in Shad. His greasy yellow hair was flopping over his face and his eyes were downcast. His teeth were chattering. His shirt front was torn and he walked as if he ached all over.

Besides his messed up appearance, Jebby sensed another difference in Shad. Something about him had changed. But Jebby couldn't put his finger on what it was. For one thing, Shad wasn't cocky anymore. And he looked so alone—not exactly frightened. But there was just this terrible aloneness that enveloped him as he was half dragged forward in the pale moonlight. For an instant, Jebby felt sorry for Shad. But the thought was a fleeting one, for Jebby wanted to banish any feelings of kindness toward the boy who had caused so much trouble. Jebby knew inside his heart—or wherever these little secret feelings hide themselves—that he felt a kind of kinship of aloneness with Shad. Of course, Jebby knew he wasn't alone in the world really. He had his mother when she wasn't working. Also he had Major MacFae and the Lama. And there was Isabella. He had her and yet he didn't have her. But Shad didn't even have this much. He lived with his married sister, he remembered Katie telling him. Nobody knew much about his mother and father. So, all Shad had was the gang—the Caps. And the only way he could hold them was by being their leader. And a leader must be strong. And to be strong to Shad was to be tough. These feelings and half thoughts retreated almost as quickly as they had come. But they left their impression.

Shad was pushed forward into the circle by Page, his proud captor. "What are you doing out here in Rock Creek Park at this hour?" Director Bush asked gruffly.

Shad didn't reply. He glanced around the circle at Major MacFae, Senator Peterson, Katie, Jebby's mother, the Zoo director, two guards and Jebby. He brushed the flopping hair back from his face. He looked straight at Jebby.

"She's a wild one, all right," he said. "I saw the whole thing."

"You mean you followed us the whole time," Jebby asked, not letting on how secretly pleased he was that Shad had seen Isabella prove her wildness and his statements in the essay.

"Yep. Sure did. Saw the whole thing." He paused as if he thought he was saying too much. Everyone waited, but Shad didn't seem to want to go on.

"Speak up, lad," the Major said briskly. "Have you got no voice to tell the story? And the truth, it jolly well might be now."

"Yeah," Shad said hanging his head. He looked as if he was trying to make a decision. Then he looked up brightly with the expression of a person who had made a decision—one that might even change his entire life.

He straightened up his shoulders. For once they looked square and strong.

"Yes sir." Shad started all over again. "I'll tell you the truth."

The Major nodded to go ahead.

"You see I wanted to get even somehow. I've had it in for Jebby ever since he gave me a bloody nose. And I guess I've had it in for you, too, sir, because you're his friend." This was one of the few times in his life Shad had said "sir" but it came out easily and naturally.

"So after the horse got loose and after what Jebby did to me, well I just thought I could get another crack at him. The other kids left. They were afraid they'd be missed at home. Nobody would miss me if I didn't come home for a week."

Shad paused to take a breath for the words were coming fast. No one spoke a word to break his mood, but he himself had broken it when he realized that he had confessed to the entire gathering that he was an unwanted boy. He quickly changed the subject from himself to Jebby.

"Pretty nice little setup you all have up there in the woods with that old fellow. What in the heck is he anyway, with robes and all?" Shad asked.

"A lama," Jebby replied. "That's a Buddhist priest."

"Well whatever he is, he sure must have some kind of magic in that tent to make you come to so fast. You was out cold, boy—really cold. That was some fall you took."

"You mean you really saw the whole thing," Jebby asked as if he were unable to accept this fact.

"Sure did. I reckon I would have come out there and pulled you up, but she—that mare—scared the daylights out of me and then when I heard those bagpipe whistles the Major here was blowing, I just lit out. I sure got to hand it to him. That was some rescue." Shad was still excited by what he had seen.

"I am sure glad that I didn't get up on that mare's back up there at the Zoo," Shad admitted.

Director Bush abruptly interrupted the boy, whose tone of voice was becoming more friendly toward Jebby.

"Well, I take it you kids weren't in cahoots about getting on this mare."

"Oh no sir," said Jebby quickly. Shad nodded in agreement.

"It will take me a little time to get all this straightened out— bagpipes, lamas and tents—but first we've got to find that mare and get her back to her pen. She's too valuable to be running loose." As he spoke, Jenkins drove up and parked his car behind the others.

"Good," said Mr. Bush, "here comes Jenkins now with the T gun."

Jebby's heart sank. He must make one last desperate try to keep the mare from being tranquillized by the T gun and also from being lassoed and maybe hog-tied. She had followed Haggis, Major MacFae and himself twice before. Even though she had been frightened away, perhaps she would follow him again and in some way he could get her back to the Zoo. He didn't know whether he could ever get her into the cruel pen again, but he would be like a Judas goat and try to get her to follow Haggis in. And maybe she would follow, for after all, it was home.

The worried boy looked at Major MacFae, whom he felt sure was reading his thoughts. The Major nodded and there was a look of confidence in his blue eyes.

"Let me try," said Jebby. "Please."

Mr. Bush looked surprised. His expression was severe. He shook his head. "No, you might be hurt—or even killed. Sorry."

"But, sir, I won't try to ride her," Jebby said. "I think she will follow me back to the Zoo. Just let me try, please."

The Zoo director shook his head again. His face was like stone. Jebby felt he was losing the battle.

Then suddenly Katie's father—Senator Peterson—spoke.

18

Second Chance

Forgive me for butting in," said Senator Peterson, "I confess I know very little about tranquillizer guns and the capturing of wild animals. But you know, Mr. Bush, I have faith in boys who have faith in themselves. This youngster believes he can get that horse back to the Zoo."

Mr. Bush did not reply, but looked surprised at the Senator's plea in Jebby's behalf.

"But," the Senator continued "the Zoo is your responsibility. If something goes wrong, you get the blame—not me. If things go well, you are the one to be congratulated—not me. Therefore, you will have to make the decision about whether Jebby goes to get the wild mare."

"Yes sir, that is right," Director Bush replied. He knew that if something went awry, he couldn't pass the blame on to Senator Peterson. He and he alone had to make the decisions, take the risks, weigh the pros and cons.

"Whatever you decide, Mr. Bush, let me take this opportunity to tell you—and I hope the others would like to hear it, too—of what this moment tonight has meant to me. It has brought into focus two problems right here in our great capital city. These are the problems of young boys and problems of the National Zoological Park. Both the boys and the Zoo need help. I think they can get that help by helping each other."

Five miles away from this ancient wooded area the Senate Chamber was empty and dark. Life had not yet begun to stir at the Capitol. The men and women who clean the corridors and offices at night had gone home and only a few night watchmen went their rounds. But Senator Peterson, his youthful face full of earnestness, didn't need his Senate desk, nor the dignity of the great Senate Chamber nor the sight of the Vice-President of the United States presiding over the session. The little open space surrounded by trees served him as well. Jebby and the others realized it.

"But let me take a moment to talk about boys. Maybe I am no authority because I have only a daughter," he grinned at Katie, "but it wasn't so long since I was one myself. Boys need a lot of things. A feeling that there is a kind but strong hand at the helm at home is one of them. But boys need to get closer to the soil and to animals. This boy, Jebby, I bet can tell us how many sets of young a mourning dove has each year, how about it?"

"Four, I think," said Jebby.

"And I bet you can tell us which day the barn swallows return to your old barn in the country. My daughter Katie told me you used to live on a farm, son."

"They come back on April 12 every year. I don't know what day they come back here 'round Washington, though," Jebby volunteered.

"My guess is that the Caps haven't worked with animals and have had little experience in the country. My guess also is that they got fed up after a while with playing games in a recreation center. They began searching for something more satisfying, but suddenly they started searching for thrills instead. For all I know they were drawn over here to the Zoo because instinctively they wanted to get closer to animals. They missed something that they had never known." The Senator paused. He wondered if he was making himself clear.

The Major broke in. "Exactly, sir. Youngsters today are too far away from other forms of life. And do you know, Senator, experience has shown me that working with animals helps to tame the man or boy."

"Every single one of us knows that our Zoo needs remodeling," the Senator continued, "needs bigger and better paddocks. Wouldn't it be fine if we could have acres of rolling green fields with several different kinds of animals in them at once? Can't you just see it?" Senator Peterson waved his arm in an arc as if he were trying to sketch in the picture. "Zebra, giraffes, ostriches, camels—and wild horses, all loose together."

Each person in the circle nodded in agreement. And the Senator seeing that they were with him in this vision of the future, went on.

"We know how important it is to preserve vanishing species of animals. Look how many have disappeared—the passenger pigeon, the great auk, the Carolina paroquet … I know you can name the ones that are threatened, Mr. Bush."

"Indeed I can," replied the Zoo director. "The European buffalo is one, the whooping crane another and even our American bald eagle. And, of course, the Mongolian horse is hard to find in the wild."

"Thank you, Mr. Bush. Now I am going to tell you what I am going to work for in the Congress of the United States. I want to see this government establish the best Zoo in the world. First, we need to remodel, in the ways I just outlined, the Zoo right here in Washington. Then we need a farm Zoo to breed and raise animals, so that fewer new animals will have to be captured and taken from their free life in the wild. And third, a junior department must be established."

Jebby, Shad and Katie smiled at these words. And the grown-ups exchanged admiring glances that Senator Peterson could have worked out such an orderly plan.

"Now, let me get the most important thing off my chest. It is more important to save wild rootless boys from a life behind bars than anything else. I believe that having boys work at this Zoo farm on weekends and in the summer would help to give them a real purpose in life. During the week afternoons they can have certain duties at the Junior Zoo right here. They can help take care of the young deer and lambs in this Zoo and tell the smaller children some of the important things they need to know about animals." He paused and glanced at Shad. "How about it, Shad? I've got a hunch you might like animals just as much as Jebby here."

"Well, I'll tell you something, Senator," Shad replied kicking at the dirt with his shoe. "I had a dog once but that drunk brother-in-law of mine kicked it around so much that it ran away. I think it was hurt and it crawled away to die. I hunted but couldn't find it. But now that I am big, my sister she tells me she don't want no dog around because it already costs too much to feed me."

This further admission of unhappiness at home came tumbling out but words were forming a bridge of understanding between him and the others. But as before when he talked about himself, he fell suddenly silent. The memory of that little mongrel puppy had haunted Shad, but this was the first time in years he had mentioned it.

Jebby sensed Shad's embarrassment about displaying his feelings in public. "Golly, Shad, Senator and everybody, these ideas are really super. Helping to take care of these animals would be more fun than working on Grandma's farm. It would be really great to work with the baby zebra."

"I'd like to help with them, too," Shad broke in. "And I seen one of them baby alpacas one time, fuzzylike. Looked like lambs to me. I'd sure like to help take care of them."

Katie looked at Jebby and smiled. When Shad said the word "lamb," Katie was sorry she had teased him about the lamb in the second verse of the poem "Tiger, tiger burning bright in the forest of the night." It was so true that God, who made the Tiger, made Shad and the Lamb, too. Now Shad knew it and was admitting it for all to see. Katie and Jebby then grinned at Shad. And then Shad grinned back. This was their secret, between the three of them. They would never talk about it, but they would never forget this moment, ever.

Though Major MacFae didn't know of the incident in English class about the Tiger and Lamb poem, he felt—from just watching the lad—that he had come a long way in a short while. Seeing Jebby get his comeuppance from the wild mare, but also seeing Jebby proved right that she was wild seemed to have taught the Cap gang leader something. Maybe he had realized that there were forces in life stronger than himself. Whatever the reason for the boy's change of heart, the Major clapped him on the shoulder. "Maybe you can help me with those Marco Polo sheep we are going to get for Mr. Bush, eh laddie?"

"Sure would, Major," he replied. "Whole thing sounds like some deal to me."

Mr. Bush was grinning broadly. "Senator Peterson," he said, "this has been my dream for years—better conditions for the animals. But it was beyond my ambitions to hope that a United States Senator would feel this way." He extended his right hand to the Senator. "Thank you, sir. That day at the hearing I felt you were with us."

"Thank Jebby Andrews," Senator Peterson replied, "not me."

He clapped Jebby on the back. "This youngster's rough experience with those other kids got me to thinking and asking questions. You know things seem different when they hit close to home. My daughter thinks highly of this lad and she made me see things I hadn't seen before."

"Senator," Jebby's mother said rather timidly. "I want to thank you, too. I guess I should have watched Jebby more closely, but I didn't realize that he wouldn't be safe at the Zoo. He kept the details away from me. He didn't want me to worry."

"Well, let's hope that everything is going to improve from now on, and Washington, with its Junior Zoo, can become a model for the country," Senator Peterson replied.

The Senator had outlined his plan for the Zoo and the boys, but he had said nothing more in behalf of Jebby having the opportunity to get the wild mare. Mr. Bush was on the spot. If the moonlight, now giving way to dawn, had been brighter, the others could have seen the red creep up around his ears. The group, relentlessly, waited for his decision about catching Isabella.

If he changed his order to hunt the wild mare with the tranquillizer gun, it would look as if he was doing it only to please Senator Peterson. But on the other hand, suppose the boy did get badly hurt or killed as he tried to get the mare to return?

It was a bad position to be in. Mr. Bush gulped as if his throat felt dry. Everyone was looking hard at him. They were waiting. Only he could say "yes" or "no."

The seemingly interminable silence was broken at last. It was Major MacFae. "Thank you again, Mr. Bush, for your good words about my books. I would like indeed to talk to you about my expeditions and the Ovis polii. I am glad you have confidence in my work." Then the old Major paused.

"I hope you have the same confidence in my word that the boy can return the wild mare to the Zoo without harm coming to

himself or her."

Major MacFae said no more. This, Jebby realized, was all that the Major could do to help him.

Jebby's mother spoke. "I think he can do it, Mr. Bush." She could say no more, but everyone knew that she had weighed her decision carefully.

Now it was Shad's turn. "I think so, too. I really do," he said earnestly.

Everyone had spoken except Katie and now her turn came. "Mr. Bush," she said clearly and firmly. "Jebby can do it. Give him a chance, please." Her gray eyes, fringed by lashes as dark and thick as Haggis' spoke more than words.

Mr. Bush was clearly outnumbered. Jebby had an overwhelming vote of confidence from people who had faith in him. If Mr. Bush didn't give the boy a chance, it could appear that he was worried more about what would happen to him as Zoo director should Jebby fail in his mission and get hurt. If the boy's mother was willing to take the risk, she was showing that she was placing more importance on giving the boy self-respect than she was on his skin. Mr. Bush realized that for a boy to live at peace with himself and respect himself was the most important thing in life. This boy wanted to do that. Jebby felt responsible for getting the mare in this mess, and he wanted to get her out of it.

"All right, Andrews," Director Bush said crisply. "I'll give you thirty minutes to get the mare back to the Zoo."

Jebby grinned through his swollen face. Even his lips were swollen from Shad's blows. Ow—it really hurt to smile, but he was willing to go through the greatest torture to show his appreciation. He would prove that he could be a friend of Isabella's and that she would follow him without the use of force. This faith that he could do it burned strong. He must save the mare. If he failed, she would be shot by the T gun or lassoed.

"Here, take Haggis," said Major MacFae stepping away from the camel's head. Jebby looked, for a moment, a little taken aback. Him, riding the camel alone? But he wouldn't refuse if that would help to bring Isabella back safe and sound. Jebby painfully climbed between her humps—he was hurting from his fall from Isabella and the fight with Shad—the way he had seen the Major do. He gave her a gentle kick in the ribs and said, as the Major had, "sook, sook, sook." He could feel a tremor go through the Bactrian camel's body. She was responding! Up she arose, rocking forward, then backward—like an earthquake in reverse.

His mother, the Zoo director, Senator Peterson, the Major, Katie, Shad and the guards and keepers watched the performance with admiration. On Katie's face there was an expression that contained even more than admiration. It was a combination of awe and affection for a brave boy who wasn't afraid to admit his mistakes. She knew he had vowed never to try to ride Isabella. He had broken that vow once, but he was willing to take the consequences.

"Good show," called the Major with encouragement in his voice.

"And good luck," added Senator Peterson.

"Say, Jebby," called Mr. Bush. "I've got an idea. If she follows you, don't take her back to the same small pen, but let's try her in the big deer pasture. Plenty of grass there. Plenty of space. Leave the old camel with her."

Jebby couldn't believe he was hearing correctly. "All he could say now was "Thank you, sir." Then he called almost gaily to the group, "I'll see you in thirty minutes, back at the Zoo—Haggis, Isabella and me." His voice was more confident than his feeling inside. He felt a little weak and fearful that his gamble—even his boast—wouldn't work.

Up the hill and around the curve and into the deepest wood Jebby rode. As he approached the little dell he could hear Dorje Lama's familiar chant.

Om ... mani ... padme ... hum ... Om ... mani padme ... hum.

The sounds were comforting, even though he still didn't know that they meant, "Hail to the Jewel in the Lotus." But this time Jebby did not pause to talk of Buddha. For as the moon rode high in the heavens and soon was to fade before the dawn, he was making his own discovery—as every boy or man must make his own discoveries.

Jebby was discovering, as the old camel ambled along at her own pace, that if you are truly sorry there is such a thing as a second chance. He had broken nature's rule by trying to ride Isabella. But now his friends, and the boy who once had been his enemy, wanted him to succeed at his chance to redeem himself. He knew in his heart—as a cardinal started up its morning song—that Isabella would give him that chance, too, by turning and following him to her new home in the Zoo.

This way they would both win. She would always be his friend in the days of green pastures ahead. But, also, the proud and gallant Isabella, would remain forever wild.

About the Author

ANN COTTRELL FREE was born in Richmond, Virginia, in 1916. A graduate of Barnard College, she became the first woman Washington correspondent for *The New York Herald Tribune, Newsweek,* and *The Chicago Sun,* where she covered First Lady Eleanor Roosevelt and wartime-Washington. After the war she served in China as a special correspondent for the United Nations Relief and Rehabilitation Administration and in Europe for the Marshall Plan. She later wrote for the North American Newspaper Alliance and was a contributing columnist for *The Washington Post, The Washington Star,* other newspapers and syndicates. In 1963 she received the Albert Schweitzer Medal from the Animal Welfare Institute for her investigative animal reporting.

The publication of *Forever the Wild Mare* brought her many other honors, including the Dodd, Mead *Boys' Life* Writing Award. She initiated the establishment of the Rachel Carson National Wildlife Refuge and presented testimony on numerous animal protection issues to Congressional committees. She was also a founder of the Friends of the National Zoo. She authored *Animals, Nature and Albert Schweitzer, Since Silent Spring: Our Debt to Albert Schweitzer*

and Rachel Carson and a volume of poetry, *No Room, Save in the Heart.*

She received the Rachel Carson Legacy Award in 1988 and in 1996 was inducted into the Virginia Communications Hall of Fame. Her oral histories are in the collections of Columbia University and the National Press Club. In 2004 she died at the age of 88 in Washington, D.C. A year later, the National Press Club Ann Cottrell Free Animal Reporting Award was established to inspire and encourage other journalists to follow in her footsteps. More information can be found at AnnCottrellFree.org.

ELISSA BLAKE FREE was born and raised in Washington, D.C., where she attended Holton-Arms School and Bethesda Chevy-Chase High School. She attended college at Ohio Wesleyan University, St. Clare's Hall, Oxford, and Macalester College. After graduation, she worked as a production assistant/ researcher in the Washington bureau of CBS News for *Face the Nation* and the *CBS Morning News*. In 1980, she joined CNN, where she held a variety of positions for 21 years, including producer, executive producer, and newsroom manager, in the network's Washington bureau. After leaving CNN, she served  as executive director of communications at Georgetown University Law Center for a dozen years. She currently works as a communications and outreach consultant and volunteer in the areas of animal protection and plant-based nutrition.

Afterword

Although the characters in *Forever the Wild Mare* were fictionalized, some had real-life counterparts:

Ann Cottrell Free, 1958

Isabella was inspired by the lone Przewalski's mare owned by the National Zoo in the 1950s and 1960s. The world's only truly wild horse, the Przewalski's are actually a separate subspecies, having 66 pairs of chromosomes, compared to 64 for a domestic horse.

Haggis was a composite of the Bactrian camels who lived at the National Zoo in the 1950s and early 1960s. My mother (center) spent time learning about them from Zookeeper Charles R. Thomas (left) and expert Georg Soderbom (right) of the Royal Ethnographical Museum in Stockholm.

                    4500 Que Lane N.W.
                    Washington 7, D.C.
                    July 14, 1963

Dear Joan and Jamie:

     Now I can tell you about "Forever the Wild Mare." For such
a long time I have wanted to, but preferred to wait until most
of the hurdles were cleared.

     You have probably guessed it. It is a novel for young people
built around the Przewalski horse.

     You will never believe this, but you are responsible in more
ways than one for the inspiration. Just before you went away for
the first of your long sojourns abroad, I lunched with you at the
Zoo, Departing, I noticed the Przewalski horse. This was my first
knowledge of this fascinating creature that is now so rare.

     From that moment on I was hooked. The book began to take
shape immediately. And my young hero, Jamie, sort of became you
at age 14. His name, however, is Jebby Andrews! (Turns out
that he was named for fellow Virginian, General J.E.B. Stuart.)

     The book has taken me down roads and footpaths I scarcely
knew existed: from the great Dzungarian gateway to the caves of
Lascaux and Altamira; to exchange of letters with leading German
and Soviet zoologists; into the land of Buddha, the problems of
ecological balances and the turmoils of social upheaval -- and, of
course, most of all into the world of story telling and our wonderful
language.

     Sometimes I had to put it aside for a year at the time while
I worked on a daily newspaper column, got into full-scale battles
on the humane front or park-saving problems. But it was always there,
my secret vice and secret love. Finally, last summer I decided to
wind up the whole thing. And then I knew what it was I wanted to say.
(And here again your interest in the world and life around us for
its own sake worked its influence. Though God knows you never pros-
elytize.)

     Dodd, Mead & Co; brings it out on October 14. And much to my
surprise it won the Dodd,Mead-Boy's Life Writing Award.

     So -- my thanks to you.

Young hero, Jebby Andrews, was loosely based on Jamie Andrews,
a friend of my mother's. She had lunch with Jamie and his wife
Joan the day she first spotted the Przewalski's mare in her pen at
the Zoo in 1958. She wrote to them before the book was published
to let them know of their important role in its creation.

Meantime, Back at the Corral . . .

Give a Man a Horse He Can Ride, But—Puleeze—Not 'Pride of the Zoo'

Nostalgia for his boyhood day on the farm, Charles Gabbert needed only a friend's bet that he couldn't ride a horse to propel him aboard the first one to come in view.

It was Trigger Gold Flash, a relative of Roy Rogers' Trigger and the pride and joy of the Zoo police.

But to Gabbert, a 25-year-old carpenter who lives at 1819 Kenyon st. nw., it was a chance to ride a horse and win a buck.

He leaped from the car in which he and his friend were driving Wednesday evening through the Washington Zoo, scrambled over an 8-foot chain fence and climbed bareback on the 9-year-old palomino thoroughbred which leads the Zoo police detachment in official parades.

"I just sat on the horse. It comes natural," Gabbert said yesterday, explaining that he was raised on a farm near Front Royal, Va.

"I rode it around the lot four or five times. An officer said what are you doing? I said I'm taking a ride on a horse. I rode it around one or two times more."

The officer, Sgt. Earl King, charged Gabbert with disorderly conduct. He pleaded guilty yesterday before Municipal Court Judge Milton S. Kronheim Jr., who suspended a $25 fine.

My mother may have gotten the idea of boys sneaking onto Zoo grounds to ride animals from a June 30, 1961, *Washington Post* article. She saved a clipping about a young man who was raised on a farm in Front Royal, Virginia, who jumped on one of the horses owned by the Zoo police force. In this case, he succeeded!

Shenandoah County, Virginia, was chosen as Jebby's home place after my mother spent time there visiting me at Camp Strawderman. The girls' summer camp is close to North Mountain, and Stoney Creek runs through the property. Both are important landmarks to Jebby.

Sen. Lister Hill of Alabama was thinly disguised as Sen. Lester Hillary in the "On Capitol Hill" chapter of *Forever the Wild Mare*. Hill was the chairman of the powerful Senate Labor and Public Welfare committee and was a senior member of the Alabama congressional delegation, whose members my parents knew quite well because my father was the Washington correspondent for *The Birmingham News*. Over the years, Hill was very helpful to my mother in her efforts to advance legislation to benefit the welfare of animals.

Katie's father, the athletic and kind-hearted Senator from Wyoming, Elias Peterson, was inspired by Senator Gale McGee who represented that state from 1959 to 1977. McGee ran for office on a platform of youth and new ideas, which garnered national support, including from former First Lady Eleanor Roosevelt. McGee served in the Senate alongside John F. Kennedy, and the two remained friends after Kennedy became President. My mother was delighted to present McGee with a copy of *Forever the Wild Mare* shortly after publication.

Zoo Director Bush of *Forever the Wild Mare* was inspired by Theodore Reed, then-director of the National Zoo. (Theodore Reed
on right, Sen. Lister Hill on left)

My mother crossed paths with Reed again when she was a witness at a congressional hearing in 1982, where she criticized a planned bow and arrow hunt of deer in fenced-in areas of the National Zoo's research facility in Front Royal, Virginia. Her efforts to stop the hunt were successful. (Ann Cottrell Free center, Theodore Reed on right)

Fictional Children's Bureau Director Bell, who testified at a Senate hearing on the problems facing juveniles in the 1960s, was inspired by Katherine Oettinger (left). Oettinger was Chief of the Children's Bureau of the Department of Health, Education and Welfare from 1957–1968. She was a pioneer in the areas of social welfare for children, and upon her death, *The New York Times* hailed her as an authority on the care and upbringing of children and an expert on mental retardation. My mother was pleased to present Oettinger with a copy of *Forever the Wild Mare* at a book party at the American News Women's Club in 1963.

Rep. Kenneth Roberts of Alabama (far right), although not fictionalized in *Forever the Wild Mare*, made complimentary remarks about it on the floor of the U.S. House of Representatives and inserted a review of the book from *The Washington Post* into the *Congressional Record*. Roberts was later persuaded by my mother to hold the first-ever Congressional hearings on the welfare of animals in laboratories, which later led to the passage of the Animal Welfare Act.

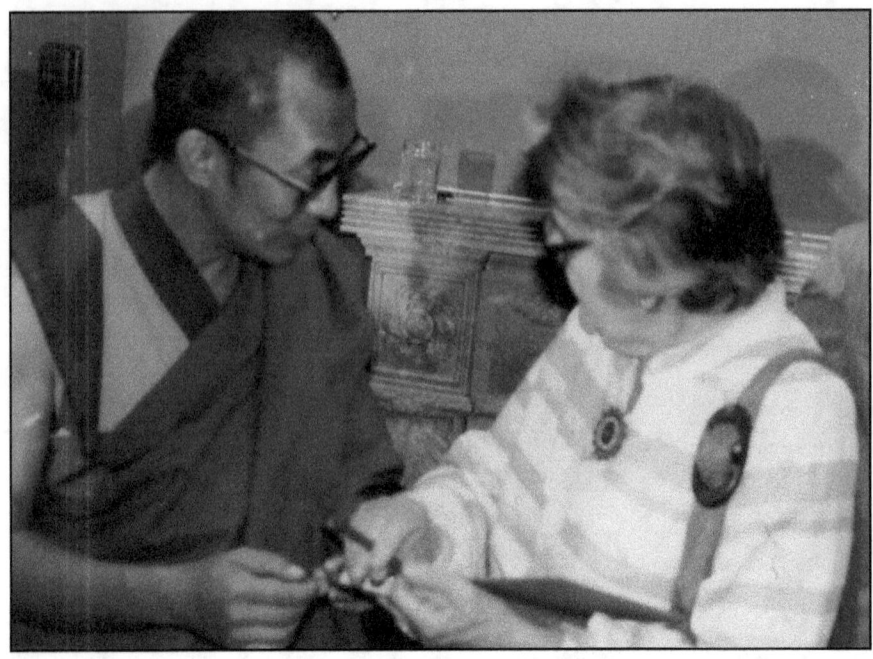

Although the 14th Dalai Lama wasn't portrayed in *Forever the Wild Mare,* he is representative of Tibetan Buddhism and, of course, the fictional Dorje Lama who played such a large part in the book. My mother was honored when she had the opportunity to present the Dalai Lama with a copy of *Forever the Wild Mare* when he visited Washington on his first visit to the United States in 1979.

The inscription read: "For His Holiness the Dalai Lama - With expression of esteem for his teachings of compassion for all living things - teachings I have tried to reflect in the book through the words of a Buddhist Lama taking refuge in Washington, D.C. (see especially chapters four and ten) - Ann Cottrell Free"

During their brief meeting, the Dalai Lama also signed a copy of *Forever the Wild Mare* which sits on my bookshelf today.

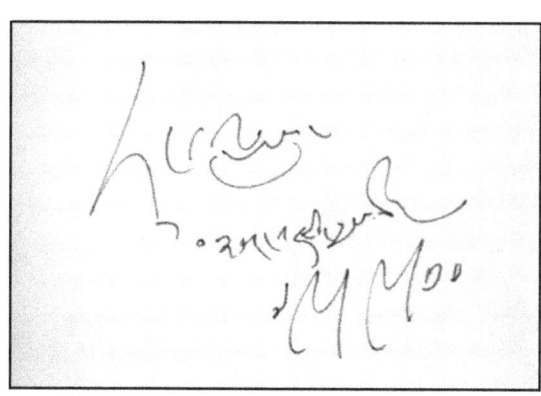

The top line is his title, Dalai Lama; the second is his real name, Tenzin Gyatso; and the third reads, September 10, 1979. (Translation by Geshe Phelgye)

Elissa Blake Free
2018

Book Notes

This section illustrates various aspects of the editorial process undertaken for the 1963 edition.

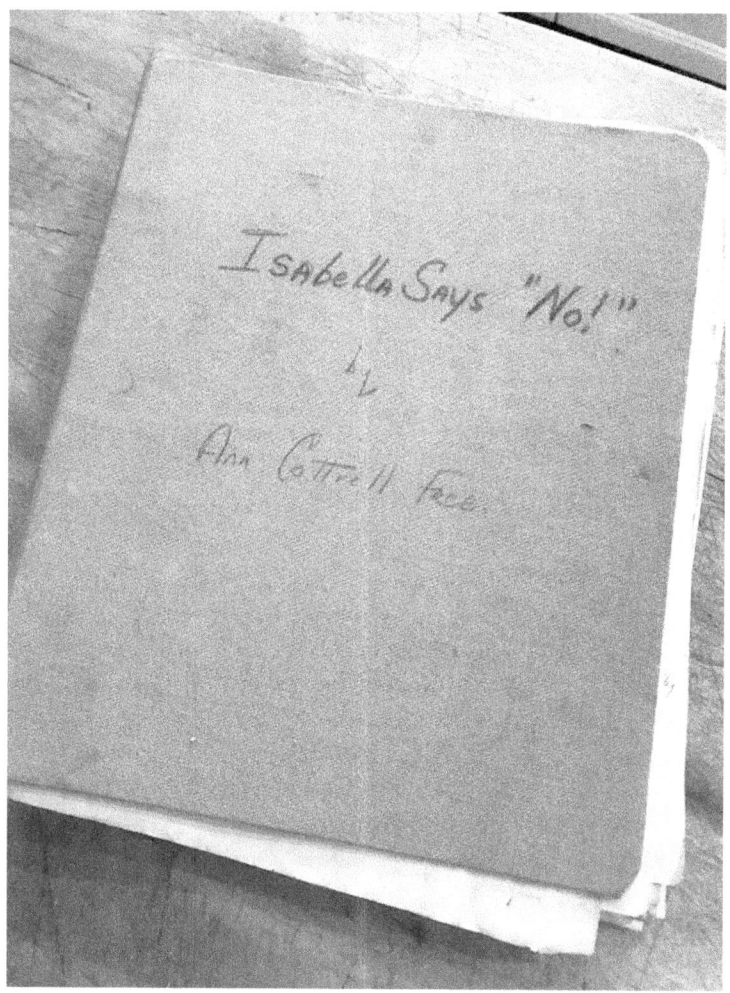

The author's original manuscript with a different working title.

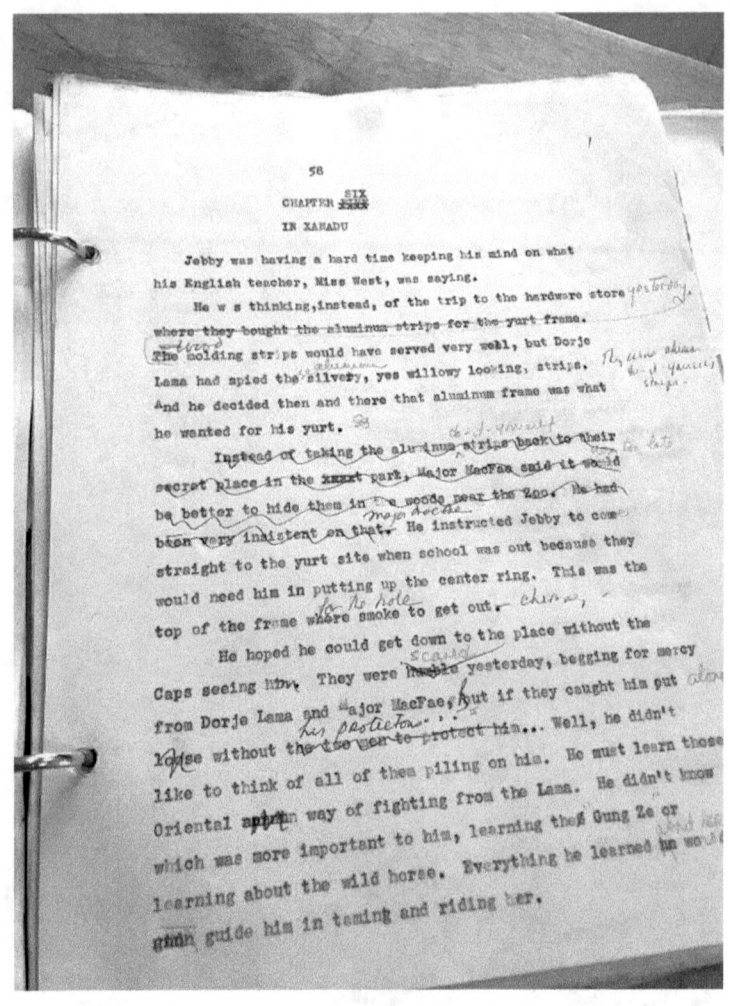

Editing in the days before word processors and computers.

> I do want to remind you, once more, that I work with a
> very soft pencil so that all changes and queries may be completely
> erased from the manuscript without harming it. However, will you
> please leave my queries in the margins of the manuscript when you
> return it to me so that I may see how you have answered my quest-
> ions, before erasing them, without having to read the whole manuscript
> all over again.

A letter from my mother's editor at Dodd, Mead & Company, points out that she worked in "soft pencil," so that edit notations could be erased from the manuscript.

> to me in small sections as soon as they are ready. Usually,
> Dodd, Mead presents every author with a careful, professional
> copyreading of his or her manuscript so as to reduce the author's
> alteration charges to as low a figure as possible. With correction
> costs to the author running to about seventy-five cents a line,
> even for the changing of a period to a semi-colon, this can mount
> up very quickly. As soon as your manuscript comes to me, I will
> read it over once more and then start it going with the copyreader
> so we will not be held up for, at least, a week or two, in order
> to have this helpful job done for your book.

In 1963, it cost 75 cents a line to make changes—that's the equivalent of $6.08 today!

The original cover for the 1963 Dodd, Mead & Company edition with art by Sam Savitt.

www.ingramcontent.com/pod-product-compliance
Lightning Source LLC
Chambersburg PA
CBHW070847120626
46556CB00002B/911